Zaraffel

Ausgabe 2/2021

Bibliografische Informationen der Deutschen Nationalbibliothek: Die Deutsche Nationalbibliothek verzeichnet diese Publikation in der Deutschen Nationalbibliografie; detaillierte bibliografische Daten sind im Internet über dnb.dnb.de abrufbar.

© 2021, Erik Eising (Hg.) via Zaraffel Gruppe Berlin
Herstellung und Verlag: BoD – Books on Demand, Norderstedt

AUSGABE 2, JUNI 2021
Autoren: Mirona C., Stella Chachali, Chen-Rui Chao, Georgios Dagkakis, Erik Eising, Tim Redfern und Rika Sakalak
Layoutentwicklung: Mirona C., Chen-Rui Chao, Erik Eising
Umschlagabbildung: Mirona C., Chen-Rui Chao, Erik Eising

Zaraffel Gruppe Berlin Kontakt:
Web: http://www.zaraffel-magazin.de
E-Mail: zaraffel@gmx.de

Titelfont ©Bloxy sowie ©Bloxy Stamped von *Mike™ Cox*; https://iprefermike.com/
Die Nutzung erfolgte mit freundlicher Genehmigung.

ISBN: 978-3-7534-6243-1

Zaraffels Vision

Du wirst dich gefragt haben, was wir damit meinen und wir werden Dir geantwortet haben, Du müsstest nur in Dich hinein gehört haben. Tausend Fragen oder ein paar weniger, selten zählt mal einer nach. Seltener noch ist eine dabei, die Dich wahrhaftig angeht. Der ganze verdammte Rest liegt sanft begraben; unterm Flickenteppich der Beruhigungsunterhaltung liegen betäubte Zweifel gekehrt neben Staubwolken, Reihe für Reihe, als wäre weiter nichts los. So ist unser Leben, reden wir uns ein und hoffen dabei doch zu oft, wir mögen es uns selbst geglaubt haben. Wir irren, weil wir wandeln. Als es der ahnungsvollen Zweifel zu viele wurden, begann sich etwas zu regen in uns. Als Bewegung zunächst ziellos, richtete Zaraffel sich zeitig auf. Dies Heft, das Du in Händen hältst, wird die Verkörperung unserer Vision gewesen sein.

Ob es der Mühe wert gewesen sein wird? Die Tätigkeit des anderen zu verstehen, unter größtmöglichen Anstrengungen zu bezeigen, was denjenigen, der mit mir in Kontakt tritt, angeht, was ihn bewegt, was ihn ausmacht: das ist es, was sich für Zaraffel wahrhaftig anfühlt. Unsere Vision ist daher die der Korrespondenz und jeder, der sie teilt, ist Teil von Zaraffel. Ob es sinnvoll gewesen sein wird? Na unbedingt, es wird sogar nichts als Sinn gewesen sein. Scheinbar ist gerade alles zu haben, wenn nicht zum Sonderpreis, dann doch wenigstens mit überaus geringem Aufwand erhältlich. Ob Charisma, Charakter, Kreativität; Wissen wurde zu Information, und damit erwerbbares Gut; Anstrengung und jegliche vorangegangene Arbeit scheinbar überwunden. Der genusssüchtige Optimismus kauft sich frei von Mühe, während er sich weiterhin einredet, jede Zukunft sei möglich, nur noch nicht eingelöst. Bloß, die Zukunft wird kein verwerteter Gutschein gewesen sein. Es benötigt Zeit, Arbeit und Strebsamkeit – Hingabe – um hinnehmbare Ergebnisse zu erzielen und sowohl das, was hinter dem Ereignis steckt als auch das, was ihm vorausgeht, ist oft deutlich bemerkenswerter.

Das einst zwingende Spiel, der eingleisige Humor, ist also ernst geworden: Nur weil neue Antworten auf alte Fragen gefunden wurden, machte sie das nicht weniger fadenscheinig. Auch das Neue hat ein Recht darauf, kritisiert zu werden, und Recht ist notwendig, da ansonsten sich die längst verschwommenen Konturen relationsloser Kategorien wie „gut" und „böse" wieder einschärfen würden. Wir sehen niemanden mehr, der darüber ein für alle Mal urteilen könnte: Allein im anhaltenden

You will have been asking yourself what this means, and we will have been answering: you just needed to listen to your own inner voice. A thousand questions – give or take a few – will have been running through your mind. You will have rarely been keeping track. Rarer still might one of these questions have truly concerned you.

The whole bloody rest has gently been buried, your doubts lying numb beneath a frayed rug of sedative entertainment, swept between piles of dust, as if nothing was really happening. That's how life is, we tell ourselves, hoping all too much that we just might believe it. We stray as we wander. Once the ominous doubts became too many, something within us began to stir. In due time emerged a movement, directionless at first: Zaraffel. The printed volume that now rests in your hands will have been the embodiment of our vision.

Will it have been worth the effort? To comprehend the work of another; to understand, even with the greatest possible effort, those who reach out to us; understanding what concerns them, what moves them, what they stand for – that is what feels truthful for Zaraffel. Our vision is thus a vision of correspondence, and those who share it deserve their share in Zaraffel. Will it have been meaningful? Without a doubt. It will, in fact, have been nothing but meaning.

These days it seems that anything can be accomplished without the slightest effort, and if not, it is for sale. Whether charisma, character, or creativity, it doesn't matter; knowledge has collapsed into mere information, and, as such, become a commodity. Honest endeavour and labour seem superseded. Hedonistic optimism buys its way out of pain, all the while believing that any future is possible if it can only be cashed-in on. The future, however, will not have been a coupon.

It takes time, labour and ambition – in a word, commitment – to achieve satisfactory results. Both what is behind the event as well as what precedes it, is more than meets the eye. The once compelling game, a one-sided humour, became serious: just because new answers were found to old questions does not mean they are less threadbare.

6

Austausch kann es noch gelingen, zwischen den Aporien des Lebens zu vermitteln.

Gott war nur mal Kippen holen, doch kam nie mehr zurück. Sein Abgang, wenn auch von schwachen Geistern und Kindsköpfen anderer Gesinnung spöttisch begrüßt, war keineswegs versuchshalber oder auf Probe. Nietzsche vermisste ihn schrecklicher als viele nach ihm. Das Ziel, die zweckmäßige Handlung indes, war auserkoren worden, diesen Verlust zu kompensieren. Entwicklung und Fortschritt, ursprünglich noch von Gottes Gnaden, sollten nun ihren einstigen Gönner ersetzen; ein Fehlentwurf. Übrig blieb allein das Ziel um seiner selbst willen – die Bedeutung solch gestalteter Industrie ist heute so hohl wie das Zeichen, dem sie entsprungen war. Wie so manches unter den Teppich gekehrt wird, wurden dabei innere Prozesse der obsessiv verfolgten Entwicklung zu Unrecht vernachlässigt.

Nun müssen wir doch feststellen, dass sich unsere Erkenntnis derselben Illusion des Untergangs verdankt. Philosophen schrieben *„causa causae est causa effectus"* und meinten damit, selbst unser Scheitern wäre nicht grundlos. Wir lassen es erst gar nicht darauf ankommen und werden noch heute tätig.

Warum, fragst du dich? Zaraffel wartet nicht in lethargischer Ewigkeit, im Komfort der glattkonstruierten Plastewelten des Digitalen. Wir müssen es tun, weil Ihr es nicht macht. Wir fühlen es auf unseren Schultern; auf unseren Armen und Beinen, auf unserer Generation lasten Generationen von Schulden, manche eingelöst und wieder andere nicht. Das meiste ist nicht Dein Problem, doch sei herzlich eingeladen, hier zu halten, die Reisekoffer stehen zu lassen und den Flug mit uns zu verpassen, sobald Du in dieser Wunderkammer voller Kuriosa einen Ansporn dazu gefunden hast. Lass mich versuchen, Dir in der Zwischenzeit aufzuzeigen, weshalb wir uns dafür verantwortlich fühlen wollen. Diese Verantwortung, welche sich für uns aus der Notwendigkeit heraus ergab, werden wir gemeinsam übernommen haben.

Mit Gott starb sowohl der Anspruch auf Moral als auch das perfekte Motto, ferner wurde die Wahrheit an sich verdächtig. An sich selbst zu denken ist als Handlung intellektuell oft notwendig und moralisch indifferent; Gemeinschaft aber entsteht nur dann, wenn für das Wesen ihrer Mitglieder gesorgt würde. Zaraffel wird denen Trost ($\pi\alpha\rho\alpha\mu\dot{\upsilon}\theta\iota$) gespendet haben, die Mitleid als einzige Triebfeder moralischen Handelns begriffen haben.

Mitleid, moderner: Empathie, ist wie jedes Wort nur Träger derjenigen Botschaft, die sein Empfänger in der Lage ist herauszulesen.

Even that which is new must be criticized; this is necessary, in fact, lest such shapeless categories as "good" and "evil" be again allowed to sharpen their edges. We no longer recognise anyone who can judge these matters once and for all. Solely in continuous correspondence lies a chance to mediate between the aporia of life.

God went out for a pack of cigarettes and never came back. His departure, even if mockingly welcomed by naïve loons and dubious minds, was anything but probationary. Nietzsche missed God dreadfully, more so than many who came after him. Compensating for that loss became, subsequently, the preeminent goal. Development and progress, once made possible by the grace of God, were to replace their former patron. A design fault. What was left over, then? Nothing but progress for progress' sake; the goal of merely having a goal. Today the significance of this endeavour remains as empty as the sign from which it first emerged. As so much is swept under the rug, the inner processes of this obsessively pursued development have been unfairly neglected. Alas, this insight we owe to the same illusion of demise.

Philosophers used to write "*causa causae est causa effectus*", whereby they meant that even our failure would not have been without reason. We do not want to take our chances, and so we choose to act immediately. Why, you ask? Because Zaraffel cannot wait in lethargic eternity, in the comfort of the constructed, plastic worlds of the digital. We have to act, because others do not. We sense a weight upon our shoulders, upon our arms and legs. Our generation's shoulders carry generations' worth of burdens, some already redeemed, others not.

Most of it is not your problem, but feel free to stay here, leave your baggage where it stands, and miss your flight together with us and allow something in this cabinet of curiosities to catch your eye. In the meantime, let us explain why it is that we want to feel responsible. This responsibility, which for us has arisen out of necessity, is one we will have been assuming together.

With God died not only the entitlement of morality but also the "perfect motto"; moreover, truth itself became suspicious. To care about one's own well-being is intellectually often necessary; morally, it is indifferent.

7

Unmittelbar geäußertes Mitleid wirkt deshalb oft künstlich, weil es selbst nichts mehr fühlt; diejenige Sprache, die man allgemein für eindeutig hielt, war längst umgewertet worden in ihr ironisch verzerrtes Gegenteil. Das natürliche Abbild des Mitleids, des sich Identifizierens, ist darum im Mittelbaren statt im Unmittelbaren zu suchen – im Text; doch mehr noch als die unmittelbare Kommunikation, steht die mittelbare als Vehikel zur Ausräumung falscher Eindeutigkeiten allein auf weiter Flur.

Wo konventionelle Sprache ebenso wie *computer-mediated-communication* zum aneinandergereihten Geschäftsverkehr belanglosester Information verkommen ist, verlautet das verdichtete Wort die Überwindung von Schluchten zwischen den einzelnen. Uneindeutigkeit auszuhalten ist der unumstößliche Gegenpol zur Fixierungssucht von Bedeutung in unserer immer komplexer werdenden Geschichte. Der Sinn, nach welchem wir streben, fällt nicht einfach aus seinen Buchstaben heraus, sondern muss innerhalb dessen, was er bedeutet, am äußersten Rand seiner Halbwertszeit, immer aufs Neue empfunden werden. Wir sind nicht naiv genug zu glauben, dieses sei ein konventionelles Problem, welches sich technisch lösen ließe.
Zaraffels responsiver Charakter verdingt sich seiner uneindeutigen Vielfalt. In einer erneuerten Literatur muss dieser Vision nach das Ineinanderspielen von Form und Funktion, ihrer historischen Entwicklungen nachspürend, bezeugt sein. Wo immer Distanzen zwischen Lesen und Schreiben überwunden werden, kommen wir zusammen, improvisieren und spielen wir. Unter solcher Definition entgeht auch dieses gedruckte Heft der Staubwüste der Beliebigkeit, allein da es sich ob seiner Materialität nicht in beliebigen Händen befinden kann; es spricht nur zu Dir und doch mit allen, die es lesen; mit allen, die es verstehen lernen wollen. Zaraffel wird sich seinem ambigen Sinn verschrieben haben.

Zaraffel hat keinen monetären Profit im Sinn, und doch verschenken wir nichts. Wir bieten nichts, das diejenigen leeren Symbole, denen wir uns tagtäglich ausgesetzt wissen, abpaust. Druckpreis und Almosen (ἐλεημοσύνη) sind das Signum dieser einzigen Politik, der wir uns qua Produkt anzubiedern bereit zeigen. Wer nichts hat, soll nehmen dürfen und wer geben will, der gibt. Es ist die Hoffnung auf das Kommende in positive Warenlogik übersetzt. Was wir euch nicht verkaufen, ist die Illusion, wir könnten uns die Druckkosten aus den Rippen scheuern.

Community, however, emerges only when we become concerned for the very being of the Other. Zaraffel will have been offering comfort (παραμύθι) to those who understood compassion as the sole driving force of moral action.

Compassion. Or, to put it in more modern language: Empathy. Like all words, it transmits only the message its receiver is able to discern. Empathy, when expressed directly and without mediation, feels often artificial because it itself feels nothing anymore; the very same language once believed to be unambiguous has long since been transvalued into its ironically distorted opposite. Self-identification, compassion's natural image, thus has to be sought in the mediate rather than the immediate – in text, where, lonelier than immediate communication, mediate communication ploughs its own furrow.

Whereas both conventional language as well as computer-mediated communication have been corrupted into the commercial traffic of utterly trivial information, the poeticised word makes known the need to cultivate these fields anew. To tolerate ambiguity is the undeniable antipole to the obsessive specification of meaning in our history that, minute by minute, becomes ever more complex. The purpose we strive for does not just fall out of its letters but requires that its meaning be felt over and over again, up to the very limits of its half-life period. We are not so naïve as to believe this is a conventional problem that could be solved technologically.

Zaraffel's responsive character serves its ambiguous diversity. In a renewed literature that follows this vision, the intertwinement of its form and function must be attested to by tracing their historical development. Wherever the distance between reading and writing can be overcome, we come together, we improvise, and we play.

According to this definition, even this printed volume escapes the desert of arbitrariness, as it cannot rest in arbitrary hands. It speaks to you only, and yet to everyone that reads it; to everyone who wishes to learn to understand it. Zaraffel will have thus devoted itself to its ambiguous purpose.

Zaraffel does not have monetary motives, yet we have no gift to give. We offer nothing that retraces those empty symbols to which we are exposed daily. Printing costs plus alms (ἐλεημοσύνη) are the signs of this single policy to which we, *qua product*, subscribe to.

Nicht allein darum wird man Zaraffel Opportunismus vorgeworfen haben. Der privilegierten Bürde unserer Handlungsfreiheit verpflichtet, belächeln wir diese Kritik herzlichst. Wir handeln heterogen, aus unterschiedlichsten Hintergründen heraus spinnen wir unsere Fäden, verweben unterschiedlichste Themen zu unterschiedlichsten Texten und Textsorten – ausschließlich bisher unveröffentlichtes Material. Dabei wird die Multiplizität unserer Einflüsse zwar von der Oberfläche unserer unterschiedlichen Erfahrungen her entworfen, gleichwohl bezeichnet der Mittelpunkt ihrer Schnittmenge jenen Grund, dessen Tiefe es gilt unter Aufwendung der größten Vorsicht zu ermessen, allmählich, rücksichtsvoll, *lentement*. Unsere gemeinsamen Koordinaten zu erkunden, wird unser Ziel gewesen sein, für dessen Umsetzung wir uns die Hilfe vieler Ähnlich-, Anders- und Weiterdenkenden ausrechnen.

Noch einmal: Was hier geschieht, erscheint uns notwendig; wir suchen, finden, haben alles und nichts. Wir wollen uns nicht politischen Richtungen oder Minderheitsdiskursen affiliieren, gleichzeitig sehen wir keinen Anlass darin, unsere historisch gewachsene Bedingtheit zu bestreiten. Privilegiert sein heißt, ein Problem ignorieren zu können. Zu jeder Tageszeit werden wir das „sowohl als auch" dem „entweder oder" vorziehen. Zaraffel ist kein Vektor, kein Pfeil, der, einmal abgefeuert, nie von seiner Bahn abkommt. An einem schönen Bahnhof auszusteigen, zu verweilen, zu lauschen, eine Kleinigkeit zu verstehen ist Zaraffel; ist: zu gleichen Teilen Ziel und Haltestelle seiner Welt. Zaraffel wird sich als radikal widersinnig beschrieben haben.

~

Mirona C.,
Stella Chachali,
Chen-Rui Chao,
Georgios Dagkakis,
Erik Eising,
Tim Redfern

Those who have little shall be allowed to take; and those who wish to give, may give. This is the hope of what is to come, translated into the logic of commodities. We will not try to sell you the illusion we could conjure up our printing costs ourselves.

Not for this reason alone will Zaraffel have been accused of opportunism. Indebted to the privileged burden of our freedom, we greet this kind of criticism with heartfelt smiles.

We act heterogeneously, spinning our threads across diverse backgrounds, interweaving different topics in and throughout different texts and genres. Unpublished material only. In doing so, the multiplicity of our influences will be reflected from the surface of our diverse experiences, sketching at the same time the heart of their coordinates, whose depth we wish to gauge gradually, considerately, *lentement*. To explore our common coordinates will have been our goal, the realisation of which we entrust to the help of many who think alike, differently, and/or beyond.

Again: What happens right here seems necessary to us; we seek, find, and have everything and nothing. We do not want to affiliate ourselves to a particular political tendency, nor to a particular minority discourse; at the same time, we cannot deny our historical contingency. To be privileged means being in the position to ignore a problem. At all times, we will prefer the „Both/And" to the "Either/Or". Zaraffel is not a vector, an arrow that, once fired off, never strays from its course. Zaraffel is to hop off at a beautiful station, to listen, to understand a nuance. It is both the destination and waystation of its world. Zaraffel will have described itself as radically preposterous.

~

Mirona C.,
Stella Chachali,
Chen-Rui Chao,
Georgios Dagkakis,
Erik Eising,
Tim Redfern

Inhalt

KRITZELEIEN   13

In unserem Hauptteil stellen die Zaraffel jeweils einen experimentellen, unveröffentlichten Text vor.

11

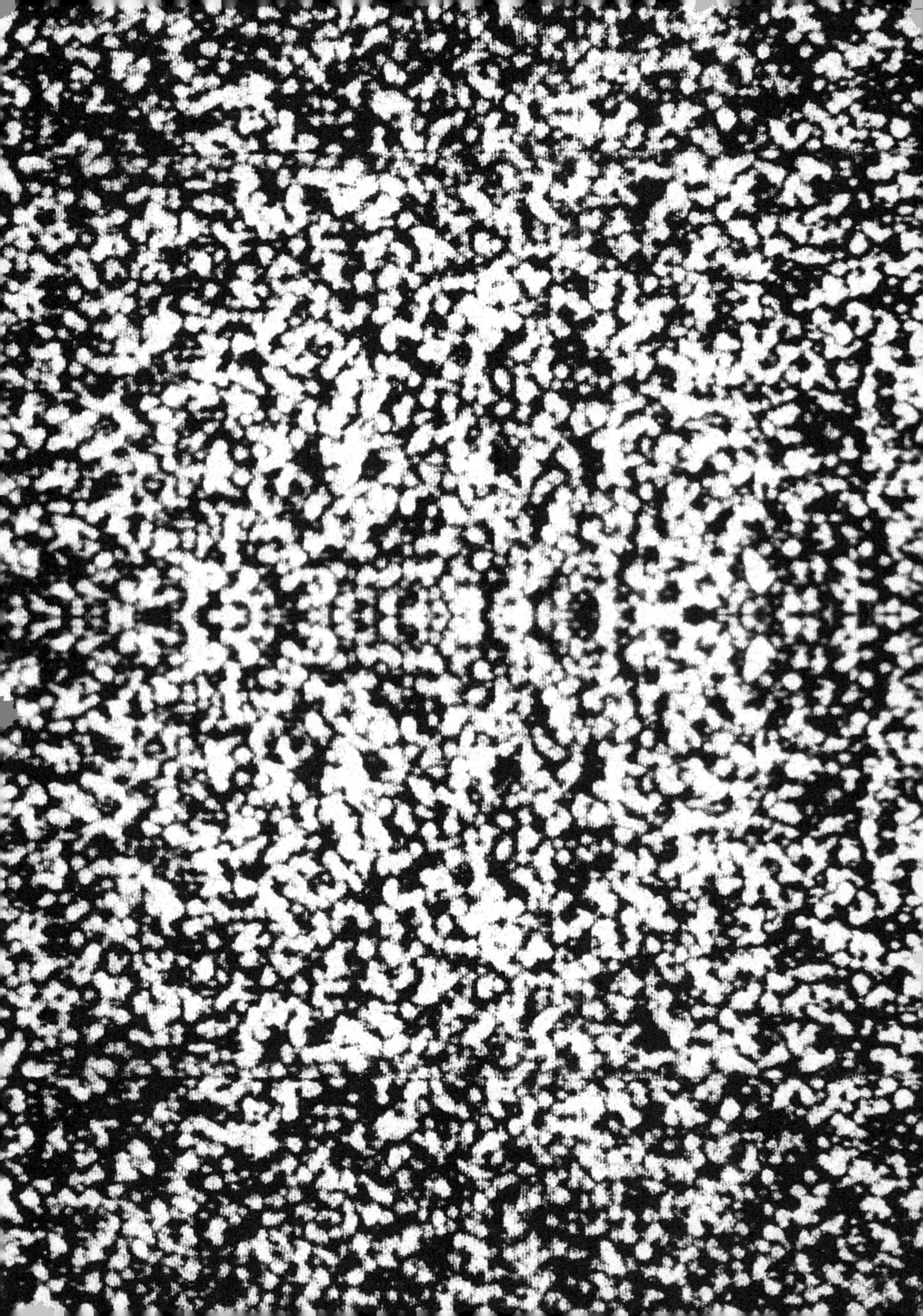

KRITZELEIEN

In unserem Hauptteil stellen die Zaraffel jeweils einen experimentellen, unveröffentlichten Text vor.

Dabei heben sich deren literarische Formen kontrastreich voneinander ab. Ist es Lyrik, Essay, Kurzepik, Comic oder Bericht?, – kein Genre wird essenziell definiert oder genießt gar einen Vorrang vor dem anderen. Hier finden sie sich alle als Kritzeleien wieder und verkörpern so, was Zaraffels Vision meint.

Während *Chen-Rui* und *Eising* jeweils den zweiten Teil ihrer Reihen liefern, tobt in Georgios Kurzgeschichte ein Krieg der Kontraste.

Sowohl persönlich als auch auf der Höhe der Zeit empfangen euch jeweils *Tim* mit seiner Erzählung und *Mirona C.* in ihrer typischen Kurzform; beide verhandeln auf ihre Art den Preis, den die Sucht ihre Protagonisten gekostet haben wird.

Um ein einzigartiges Geschenk hingegen geht es, wenn in *Stellas* lyrischen Passagen ganz eigene, sanftere Töne angeschlagen werden.

Praxissemester in Retrospektive: Teil 2

0. Vorwort

Der nachfolgende Bericht wurde im Sommer 2018 so, wie er hier steht, vom Autor als Teil des Portfolios zum Praxissemester an der Universität Potsdam abgegeben, und von der damaligen Seminarleitung überaus positiv rezipiert; das ist keine Selbstverständlichkeit, da der gewählte Tonfall, seinem literarischen Genre gemäß, mindestens ungewöhnlich, eher doch als überaus merkwürdig gelten mag. Dabei sollte er vor allem die Kritik an der akademischen Praxis der „Reflexion" in süffisantem Ton parodieren. Sein salbungsvoll pathetischer Anstrich passt normalerweise nicht an die Universität, doch insgeheim und recht eigentlich, wenn man es peinlich genau nimmt, passt er hier…

Aufgrund seines Alters und seiner nach Fertigstellung unberührten Belassenheit, lösen einige Formulierungen beim Autor nachträgliches Stirnrunzeln aus, aber das muss ja nicht für Dich gelten und im Rückspiegel erscheinen Dinge bekanntermaßen oft größer, als sie es tatsächlich sind.

Der Bericht ist trotz allem als erster Schritt zur übergeordneten Entwicklung eines Duktus zu verstehen, der sich der Retrospektive selbst einschreibt, weshalb der Autor bescheidenerweise anmerken lässt, die bisher singuläre Leserschaft zu erweitern, sei ein erbauliches Anliegen und die nachstehenden Zeilen einem größeren Publikum zum Vergnügen bereitzustellen ein ganz und gar redliches Verdienst in eigener Sache (er wünscht also viel Spaß). Um den Lesefluss etwas zu erleichtern, wurden die fachwissenschaftlichen Passagen in der vorliegenden Version ausgespart.

(Anm. des Autors: Es folgt die Fortsetzung zum in Z1 erschienenen ersten Teil)

3. Es wird wärmer

Wie wir sehen verbat das kühle Becken dem Autor nicht die Freude an seinen ersten Schritten als zukünftige Lehrkraft; gar mit „Hand und Herz" möge der Pädagogik-romantiker säuseln, wenn er, morgens an Bushaltestellen stehend der Kirschbäume Knospen treiben sieht, um direkt in den Moloch des Schulbusses sich hinzuwerfen; mit Kopfhörern und einer Lieblingsmusik im Ohr lässt es sich ertragbar machen, den Schülern offen zu zeigen, dass auch erwachsene Menschen mit dem öffentlichen Nahverkehr unterwegs sind. Die Kollegen würden dem Autoren den Vogel zeigen, der aber findet: *ça va.*

So nimmt irgendwie alles seinen Gang. Die innere Karte zeichnet jetzt bereits den Weg von Raum zu Raum vor, die Zeit wiegt nach und nach, und doch plötzlich gängige Abläufe in Gewohnheit, sie wandelt Handeln in Erfahrung, in Erinnerung. Nicht auf anderem Wege entfalten sich Überdruss und Selbstgefälligkeit, doch für diese Eigenschaften sich zu entwickeln bedarf es mehr Zeit als dieses Praktikum zur Verfügung stellen sollte und überdies auch mehr Verantwortung. Aus jener Perspektive lässt sich der nun folgende entworfene und protokollierte Teil des Portfolios einklänglich betrachten. Der Autor lässt sich zwischenzeitlich verabschieden und hofft indes auf ein Wiedersehen in Abschnitt 3.4.

(Anm. des Autors: Die Punkte 3.1-3.3 wurden in der vorliegenden Fassung ausgespart.)

3.4 Freischwimmer

Mit der absolvierten Hospitation in Französisch war plötzlich sämtlicher Druck von mir genommen. Es war nicht die Angst hier zu versagen, sondern das Gefühl der Bangigkeit, das mich im Französischunterricht zeitweise ein wenig hinter eigenen Erwartungen zurückließ. Bevor ich jedoch meine Beichte zum entsprechenden Tag ablege, muss unbedingt darauf hingewiesen werden, dass das anschließende Auswertungsgespräch, insbesondere das Protokoll dazu, eine wichtige Hilfe für die Aufarbeitung und auch die Gestaltung neuer Unterrichtsstunden (vgl. 3.2.) gewesen ist.

Ich sagte bereits, dass vor der Hospitationsstunde eine bestimmte Last auf meinem Schaffen lag, die sich mit der Bangigkeit beschreiben lässt, welche mich während des Monats Mai hatte treiben lassen. Das Treiben ist der Mann'schen Mittelmäßigkeit zuzuordnen, die auch mal von Roland Barthes mit der Dummheit in Verbindung gebracht wurde. Es beschreibt das apathische Aufsichzukommenlassen einer Begegnung, in der es gesellschaftlich legitim wird zu verlangen, die betroffene Person möge sich behaupten und rechtfertigen. In der Folge ergibt sich dies Sorgenkind des Lebens immer neuen kindisch dekadenten Prokrastinationsausbrüchen; es beginnt zu treiben, mit der klaren Ahnung von Desaster auf sich zu rollend, von weit her, aus den Tiefen einer Selbstzerstörungswut mit 1898 Bar Druck, von der es jäh ans Licht gerissen werden wird.

Ganz wie ein berühmter Korken auf der Wasseroberfläche, drückt er sich. Doch die Geschichte beginnt ja erst: Am Tag vor der Hospitation begann ich, aus hinlänglich genannten Gründen, meine Unterrichtsstunde zu planen. Aufgrund der mangelnden Zuträglichkeit seitens meines Mentoren war mir schon seit Beginn bewusst, dass ich diese Stunde irgendwie aus dem Ärmel schütteln werde müssen; lästigerweise hatte er plötzlich Interesse, mir ausgerechnet bei dieser Stunde helfen zu wollen, was mich vor ein Problem stellte: Wie mochte ich dem Mann klarmachen, dass ich am Wochenende vorher nicht in Berlin sein werde (aufgrund einer Familienfeier), ohne damit seinen Zweifel an meiner *dédication* zu ködern (ein Haken, auf den er schon seit meiner ersten Stunde wartete wie ein Hai, der um ein argentinisches Rettungsboot kreist)? Es ging nicht. Also ignorierte ich ihn zuerst ein bisschen und stellte ihn dann vor unvollendete Tatsachen; der kooperative Teil der Stunde wäre niemals an ihm vorbeigegangen, allein aus seiner Einschätzung des Gelingens einer nicht frontalunterrichtdominierten Unterrichtsstunde in dieser Lerngruppe heraus. Mir war klar, dass die Methode murksen würde, weil sie an Vorbereitung kränkelte: Ich hatte sie noch nie mit den Schülern geübt, was in Hospitationsstunden für mehr Kammerflimmern sorgt, als einer tiefengespannten Person lieb sein konnte.

Zusätzlich war der komplette Rest auch Murks. Allem voran, weil die geliebte didaktische Klammer fehlte, was mir während der Planung ebenfalls klar gewesen war. Warum nur diese selbstausgesuchte Hölle? Weshalb auch all der Vorlauf?, fragt man sich zurecht. Es war so: Wie bereits erwähnt, kam ich aus einem übermüdenden Wochenende mit zirka 14 Stunden Fahrtzeit und einer leichten Beklemmung mit Blick auf den kommenden Mittwoch; ich hatte schließlich noch fünf Stunden vorneweg zu planen. Im Nachhinein ist es mir daher möglich, eine kohärent wirkende Kette von Ereignissen zu fingieren, die meinen zeitweisen Verlust von Vernunft hier in Rechenschaft rahmt.

Ich vergaß nämlich am Dienstag meinen Schlüssel in der Schule und konnte somit erst 18.00 Uhr mit der Planung beginnen. Aus der Not heraus plante ich, eine Stunde früher zur Schule zu fahren, um wenigstens den Unterrichtsraum so zu präparieren, dass möglichst viel Zeit bei den Übergängen gespart würde; doch daraus wurde nichts. Es gelang mir am Morgen tatsächlich, die falsche S-Bahn zu nehmen, mit der ich eine Station ab ███████ in die Falsche Richtung fuhr. Das kostete mich insgesamt derartig viel Zeit (nicht zu reden vom Stress, den es auslöste), dass ich kaum später als üblich auftauchte und mir weniger Zeit übrigließ, als ich normalerweise gewohnt war. Alles in allem hätte die Stunde besser laufen können, das bewies ich mir selbst in den kommenden Wochen.

Ich begann gezielter Stunden zu planen, versuchte die Gruppe und mich häufiger an schülergesteuertem Unterricht und begann im Englischunterricht Stunden zu improvisieren, also frei zu schwimmen.

3.5   Hitzefrei

Das Konzept des verkürzten Unterrichts trug seinen Teil dazu bei. Dabei wird jede Schulstunde zu einer halben Stunde, was den Blockunterricht um 30 Minuten kürzt. Meine Stunden waren daher plötzlich drei Wochen wert. Das Beste daran war, dass mir die verkürzten Arbeitstage auch die benötigte Zeit zum Planen weiterer Unterrichtsstunden verschafften, denn als meine Englischmentorin mich Anfang Juni darum bat, ihre Klassen während ihrer Abwesenheit (sie leitete den Spanienaustausch) zu übernehmen, dachte ich an alles andere als abzulehnen.

Es war ein schönes Gefühl, allein vor der Klasse zu stehen, ja, doch vor allem wollte ich mir selbst beweisen, diesen Beruf, sein Stundenpensum und die Planung von Arbeitsprozessen bewältigen zu können, und das tat ich. Das Praktikum bot mir in diesen Tagen dafür die nützlichste Probefläche.

Abgesehen davon war während der letzten drei Wochen vor allem mein Französischblock am Mittwoch gefährdet, von marodierenden Abschlussklassen, und wurde zweimal gesprengt.

Das fand ich sehr sozial von Seiten der Schulleitung; allein es bleibt systemkritisch bedenklich, dass Jugendliche in derartiger Intensität die Institution Schule in eine gesetzesfreie Zone verwandeln. Folgen wir einem elliptischen Gedankengang hierzu, möchte man jenen Umstand zu dem Schluss deuten, die Schüler nähmen Schule als Gefängnis wahr. Dabei käme Bildung das Zeichen einer Form von Gewalt zu, was mich ernstlich nachdenklich stimmt. Den Wert von Erkenntnis zu untergraben ist das Anliegen von Machtmonopolschaffenden, ganz egal in welcher Form diese auftreten. Die Begrenzung von Bildern, die Selektierung dieser, ist eine Praxis repressiver Ideologien, die sich Wissensverwässerung zum Ziel machen. Meine durchaus konservative Sorge ist der Unmöglichkeit eines kritischen Umgangs mit Massenmedien geschuldet, den schon klügere Köpfe als ich fürchteten: Ich sehe mich da in guter Gesellschaft. Soviel einmal zur Ellipse.

Alles in allem war während der letzten Wochen vor Ende des Schuljahres kein Bildungs-auftrag mehr erkennbar... wirklich gar keiner. Ging man die Schulgänge während einer Freistunde entlang, sah man durch die gläsernen Wände Schüler, die Dokus, Youtube-videos und „Der mit dem Wolf tanzt" glotzten. Wenigstens habe ich es noch geschafft, rechtzeitig die Küche zu buchen, um *mousse au chocolat* mit den Achten zuzubereiten. Das war das pädagogische Highlight meiner vorletzten Woche im Praktikum.

4. FerienGefühle
Der Schwabe tät sage: Haidenai! Jetzt sind schon alle dreieinhalb Monate vorüber und es wird die Sanduhr wieder umgedreht und der Lehrer zum Studenten; ganz zum Vergnügen des Autors, der sich im Gegenlicht dessen, auf seine Klaviatur hämmernd, verjüngen mag.
Das Spiel ist ausgespielt, die Bühne, die Publikumsränge wieder leer, einzig das Skript muss noch geschrieben werden, nachträglich, weshalb sich der Autor hier nicht wenig bemühte, den letzten Erinnerungen nachzustellen, auf dass sie ihr Geheimnis jeweils feilbieten, pünktlich zum Zeilenumbruch;
für den nächsten Auftritt, der ganz bald schon folgen wird, hoffentlich.

Schrieb ich Erinnerungen? Vielleicht... dem Autor sei gedankt für diesen magischen *rappel*, der in den folgenden, finalen Absätzen seiner Erzählung weiterhin so tun wird, als sei hier nichts als die Wahrheit am Werk. Doch so glaube mir, lieber Leser, nichts anderes wird hier geschrieben stehen. Auch wenn ich berechtigte Zweifel daran hege, dass Erinnerungen immer die Realität abbilden, doch was soll's, dafür gibt es ja Protokolle, nicht wahr?

Das Gefühl in die Sommerferien zu gehen erinnerte mich abschließend noch einmal an vergangene, eigene, Schultage; Tage, an denen noch lange nicht an die Transformation zu denken war, durch die ich heute meinen Blick von der anderen Seite des Tisches zu werfen in der Lage bin. Das Gefühl am Anfang der Sommerferien war eines der Selbstermächtigung, war ein Trugbild der Postmoderne, vielleicht. Meine Erinnerungen an die Kindheit, an die Zeit, in der ich die Schwüre leistete, die umzusetzen es im Beruf einmal galt, verblassen; allein dieses Gefühl gibt mir wieder Antrieb, wovon ich bald einigen gebrauchen kann, an kalten Tagen.

(Anm. des Autors: Die Punkte 4.1-4.2 wurden in der vorliegenden Fassung ausgespart.)

4.3. Abschließende, kritische, Anmerkungen, offene Fragen
Im Rahmen dieses Praktikums sind mir einige Fragen offengeblieben: Wieso verspricht sich der Lehrbeauftragte im Schulpraktikum, insbesondere im Fachseminar Englisch, derart viel Erfolg von erzwungener Leistungserfassung, und wie um alles in der Welt soll ein nebenbei berufstätiger Studierender sich dieses Praktikum leisten können? Diese beiden strukturellen Probleme bringen zum einen Motivation und zum anderen den Studienverlauf zum Erlahmen und sollen hier abschließend kritisch perspektiviert werden.

Wie ich bereits oben erwähnte, wäre es mir ein Vergnügen gewesen, mein Portfolio im Fach Englisch zu schreiben (auch, um ██████████ ein bisschen Arbeit zu sparen), doch sind dort die Anforderungen derart überzogen, dass ich es habe sein lassen. Wer bis hierhin gelesen hat, dem wird einleuchten, dass ich dabei nicht etwa von irgendeiner Seitenzahl spreche, sondern von den erforderlichen Einverständniserklärungen, etwa zum Videografieren von Unterricht, dem erzwungenem „Tandembesuch" an einer anderen Schule, dem Angeben einer privaten Handynummer (E-mail reicht nicht, nein). Da sich darüber hinaus das Gerücht im Umlauf befindet, die entsprechende Lehrperson hätte privat mehrfach unangemessen Kontakt mit Studentinnen des Seminars aufgenommen, ist es nicht verwunderlich, weshalb sich Zweifel über die Einhaltung der Datenschutzrechtsverordnung an der Universität Potsdam auftun.

Doch das ist nicht der hauptsächliche Unmutsgrund: Die Tatsache, dass es in der Leistungsanforderung keine individuellen Anpassungsmöglichkeiten gibt, ist es. Sicherlich, an meiner Schule war es kein Problem auf alle erforderlichen Stunden zu kommen, doch ich habe auch von Kommilitonen gehört, die trotz mehrfacher Bitte an ihre Mentoren keine Unterrichtszeit, und damit ein *per definitionem* zweckloses Praktikum absolvieren mussten – in der Hoffnung, dass wenigstens das Dokument von den Verantwortlichen unterzeichnet würde. So qualifiziert es sich im Zweifelsfall eben. Dieses Vorgehen hat einen triftigen Grund, auf den ich sofort zu sprechen komme, doch hier noch ein Tipp: die Kommunikation mit den Schulen muss besser werden. Es darf keine ungeeigneten Mentoren mehr geben, es darf einfach keine empathielosen Ausbilder an solch empfindlichen Lupenstellen der Lehrerausbildung geben. Keine Freiwilligenbasis, sondern Abminderungsstunden; Qualität darf kosten. Es ist klar, dass es sich hierbei um eine politisch motivierte Angelegenheit handelt.

Aber warum genau würde ein Kommilitone nach einem nutzlosen Praktikum nicht wenigstens Lärm machen und darauf bestehen, zu unterrichten? Nach einer gewissen Zeit, die man sowieso mit Hospitieren verbringt, ist es praktisch nicht mehr möglich, die Schule zu wechseln, was das Nachholen zu erbringender Unterrichtszeit erschwert. Gleichzeitig kann das Praktikum vom Betroffenen auf keinen Fall wiederholt werden, weil es finanziell gesehen mitunter einen tiefen Einschnitt in die Lebensumstände der Studierenden bedeutet. Man kann nicht einfach so das Praktikum im nächsten Semester wiederholen, und genau auf dieser Furcht baut der gesamte Betrieb auf, was nicht nur mich zum Schäumen bringt.

Mit preußischem Arbeitseifer wird Studierenden vorgeschrieben, sie hätten soundso viele Stunden zu absolvieren – bitte bloß nicht fachfremd. Genau das ist, je nach Schule und Schulform und Fächerkombination, aber alles andere als eine zweckorientierte Anforderung. Einer meiner Kommilitonen hat mit der Schule unter der Hand fest ausgemacht, dass er mittwochs nicht anwesend sein wird, ganz einfach, weil er auf Arbeit muss. Nun steht aber im Anforderungsprofil, dass der Praktikant jeden Tag zumindest für vier Stunden an der Schule anwesend zu sein hat. Beeinträchtigt es die Qualität der Ausbildung etwa derart, wenn mein Kumpel seine Miete verdient, während er, wie jeder andere auch, hier keinen Pfennig bekommt, obwohl er theoretisch gesehen schon eine ausgebildete Lehrkraft ist?

Es gibt Beispiele *en masse*, wo Masterstudierende Lehrposten über Jahre besetzen, weil es grundsätzlich eine billigere Angelegenheit für den Arbeitgeber ist. Wenn wir hier im Umkehrschluss also für lau arbeiten sollen (und das wird uns noch als sagenhafte Chance auf mehr Erfahrung verkauft; als List des Odysseus gewissermaßen), dann sollten die Anforderungen wenigstens dynamisch sein. Es ist für Studierende aus sozioökonomisch schwachen Elternhäusern erwiesenermaßen schwieriger, ein Studium abzuschließen, da braucht es einzig einen Blick in die Statistiken der Hochschulabsolventen zu wagen. Die Hochschulen sind ein Ort des gutbürgerlichen Milieus, ein Heiratsmarkt für die Kinder von Ingenieuren. Welchen ökonomischen und gesamtgesellschaftlichen Nutzen kann es also haben, es genau denjenigen unter den Studierenden schwerer zu machen, die diese Milieugrenzen zu überschreiten wagen? Noch ein Tipp: Bezahlungsmodelle weiter-entwickeln; die Studierenden zusätzlich als Vertretungslehrer anstellen und dabei dann meinetwegen ein paar Groschen sparen; aber bezahlt doch gefälligst denjenigen, der arbeitet. Manche leben davon.

Erkennt man diese Schranken und umgeht sie, anstatt auf sie zuzutreiben wie einige, deren Unmut ich seit Erstellen dieser Zeilen mit mir trug, ist das Schulpraktikum eine wunderbare Erfahrung, ist es ein Raum zur Entfaltung, zum Experimentieren und zur Selbstermächtigung – wenn man sich ihn zu schaffen weiß. Dazu gehört an vielen Stellen eine kühne Frechheit, die der Autor im hier vorliegenden Text auch sprachlich äußerst aufdringlich zu bewerben versuchte: Es möge ihm verziehen sein.

~ Eising

Pawns

The soldier woke up. He had a bitter, stiff taste in his mouth, like the one you get when you have drunk a lot of low-quality wine the night before, yet he knew that there was no alcohol consumption involved in this case. He felt thirsty, in need of a glass of cool water, but for some reason he lit a cigarette instead. He had this strange dream once again; he would see it over and over almost every night, sometimes more than once. It was beautiful while it lasted, however it did leave this bitter taste in his mind when he was up. *Can one have a hangover because of a dream?* he wondered.

"Hello Delta, how are you today?" the Bishop's voice interrupted his thoughts; and what a nice voice it was, a trace of hoarseness was betraying his older age and in parallel his wisdom, while the way he delivered his words gave to Delta a mixed impression of kindness and severity. Anyway, Delta believed that the Bishop was a good man, always friendly despite his obvious higher position.

By the way, Delta was the soldier's nickname; it came from the fourth letter of the greek alphabet and was given to him mainly because when the war started he was positioned in area D2, where stayed there for some period, until he moved to area D4. Sometimes his friends called him just "D", sounding like "Dee", which was kind of a shorter nickname for Delta. Having a nickname on top of his nickname somehow bugged him sometimes, even more because he felt that somewhere behind all this he should have an actual name that, nonetheless, he could not recall. It must have been something he had before the war, but this *before the war* notion bugged him even more.

"I am good sir thank you, how are you?" he replied politely to the Bishop, who was camping in the adjacent area C4.

"I am fine dear Delta, thanks to God. Sitting here, doing my precious work, and waiting as we all do"

"Yes, this waiting is really something. It can get into your nerves", Delta in reality meant to say this to himself and it was too late when he realised, he did it out loud.

"I know it is difficult my good fellow Delta. You know, I heard you had a restless night again yesterday", the Bishop said and Delta regretted having opened such a discussion. This stupid dream was a real torture. He often felt the urge to talk about it and maybe the Bishop, being a religious person, would be an appropriate receiver of such confessions; however, he never found the courage to touch this issue. "All this idle time is not easy to shallow. This is why we should remain alert yet quiescent, always having faith in God first and then in our great King. The war needs strategy, and He knows best how we should proceed".

Although he would never contradict the above statement, deep inside Delta did not have much faith in the King, so he tried to change the subject. "Probably it is also annoying to see the enemy moving in such slow and insidious ways. They do look a bit frightening having this black colour", he cried and again he immediately regretted it; on the one hand he did not want the Bishop to consider him a coward and, on the other, he did not fancy sounding like a racist either.

"Sure, they are uncivilized savages", the Bishop exclaimed firmly. "This is why it is of absolute importance to win this war my little Delta. Not only for us here and now, but for the whole world and history", he added pompously.

"What do you think will happen at the end of this war?"

"Is there any doubt? We will win of course."

"Yes, of course, my question was about after that. What will it be like after this war ends with our triumph", he tried to hide any trace of hesitation.

"Ah, we will live in beautiful peace of course. Like we did before the war".

Before the war. The sound of it produced again a feeling of nausea and the following question came almost silent out of his mouth: "And how was this?"

He noticed that the Bishop looked awestruck for a while, as if the question was sensitive to him in the same way that it was for Delta; it was only for an instant, just a tiny moment, yet Delta was sure he saw it. Then the Bishop quickly regained his stable and majestic posture. "In prosperous green fields and sunny days! People laughing and enjoying family life, friendship, love, and carefree days, away from all current hardships. Ah, this war has lasted too long that it seems it is here forever, but do not worry, it will come to its end and we will enjoy peace with the love of God and under the ruling of our great King".

Delta had noticed that the Bishop always mentioned God and the King together, most of the time in that order, sometimes also in the inverted one, but in any way they always appeared combined in his sentences. Rather than that, he did enjoy his short description of sunny and colourful days; he was getting totally sick of these black and white surroundings of the battlefield. On the other hand, he did feel that the Bishop just gave a generic answer, the type that he himself could also produce if asked. And then there was this flicker in his eye, he could not be wrong.

"Mr Bishop, I would like to ask a question, how did you come to be a bishop?"

"Huh? What do you mean?"

"Nothing really. I meant to ask if it is something you wanted to do since you were a child, if you attended some specific school for this and things like that". He put his questions in a casual tone, hoping that he would not sound impolite. He was thankful that the Bishop was always open and ready to skip formalities;

up to a point at least.

"Ah, my dear soldier, I was born a bishop!" This time his voice showed no hesitation and Delta thought that he was already alarmed by the previous discussion. Delta must have looked a bit dubious, so his interlocutor continued, "do not look surprised, this is how the world works, I was created as a bishop, you were as a soldier, a very good one, but a soldier, the King as His Majesty etc". Delta was about to contradict that, when suddenly the Knight made a jump above their heads with his beautiful white horse, which made him stop. "See this?" the Bishop continued taking advantage by his silence, "could you or even I make such a magnificent move? Of course not, but *he* can: he was *born* a knight"

Delta looked at his superior; he had to admit that he did look born in a higher class than him. First of all, he was almost twice his height and Delta was not really a short guy; on the contrary, he had similar height with all other soldiers he had met. Furthermore, he had to admit that the Knight looked as if he was out of this world, he was almost flying with that stallion of his. On the other hand, even Plato said that people born in a lower class can go to the upper ones if they are worthy and, most important of all was that vision; that strange visitor in his sleep, which more than a dream felt like a memory; surely it was closer to a recollection than all the haze that occupied his brain regarding *before the war*.

"You know sir, with all my respect, but I have to say that I am not sure about that."

"What do you mean Delta?" he sounded again a bit alarmed.

"This eternal order of things... I do not know how to put it..." he started clumsily and then he realised that he had no solid rational argument, thus he decided to play the card of metaphysical experience. "You know, I have a dream. A recurring one. Sure, it is when I am asleep, but it is more real than any other dream or nightmare, I would call it a vision, one that I have every night, sometimes multiple times, this is why my sleep is so restless. I see that... No, no... I experience that..." he was hesitant now, but there was no way back, "I am the Queen!" he said it.

For a moment, the Bishop remained silent; this gave Delta all the time he needed and more in order to regret his confession and anticipate several possible reactions by the recipient. However, in the long and thorough list of potential responses his brain made, he failed to include what actually happened. "Well, I have to go", the Bishop declared plainly, as if Delta had not laid anything needing a reply. "I did not tell this to you earlier, but yesterday I got an order to go to Area E2 for a very important secret mission," he explained and then, without further words,

22

he gathered his few possessions and departed. Delta was left alone and numb. He did not believe for a moment that the Bishop's departure was uncorrelated with his own dramatic confession. He could feel the hidden contempt in his voice as he announced that he was about to leave. Neither did he believe about this abrupt secret "order" that had supposedly arrived before. No, the Bishop decided himself to leave, unlike the soldiers that had always to follow orders for every little move they made (*like pawns*, Delta sometimes thought), probably he was in position to take his own initiatives. So he made up his mind to go to E2; that was not like some move towards the enemy camp, trying to learn something or organise an attack; it was rather going back to the headquarters in order to report. To report about what? A crazy soldier, much probably homosexual, that had schizophrenic visions about being the Queen. Oh god, Delta was feeling so embarrassed, he knew that everyone would laugh their hearts out when hearing about this petty soldier; and this was only the first part; then they would start thinking how much such a soldier can be trusted in such a crucial war. He thought that he had become the first candidate for the next suicide mission that the great King would come up with.

Yet, he believed that he was not crazy; sure, this is the motto of every wacko, one cannot be sure for his own mental state. For what it's worth, he knew more positively that he was not homosexual; not that he considered being gay as something bad, besides he did not want to be conservative, and he did not have problems with the sexual orientation of others. He cherished women and he was one hundred percent aware of this, because he liked the Queen. From the very first day of the war, when he was back in D2 and the Queen stood so close to him in D1, he would always try to secretly turn his head towards her and take a precious glimpse of her beauty. Though it was always just for a fleeting moment (he would not dare more), it was enough to brighten his day. She was so elegant and refined; much taller than him (even taller than the Bishop!), which was always discouraging for Delta, who aspired to find the nerve to approach her. But what could he do, casually turn back, look at her meaningfully and tell her something like *hey*? That would be so ridiculous; and how else could it be, when an absurd, little, negligible soldier addresses himself to her Majesty the Queen? Moreover, next to her there was the King; equally tall and sufficiently frightful, even though he was way older and uglier than her. Later, Delta was moved to D4, so he wasn't close to his beloved anymore, but he never forgot her; she was in his thoughts when he woke up, when he shaved, while he was eating, generally in every breath. Sometimes he heard news about her related to the battle and they were always stories praising her skills and courage; recently they said that she alone demolished one of the enemy's towers.

Yes, he was in love with the Queen. Maybe this would be the reason for his dream, he thought; except he knew that this did not make much sense, because it would be more logical to see that he was *with* the Queen, but in his dream he saw that he *was* the Queen.

While he was lost in the above thoughts, he noticed a small envelope in front of his feet. This must be from the headquarters, he thought, but he had no idea about how it magically appeared out of nowhere. He opened it having a very bad feeling, a premonition which was very soon confirmed. *The soldier of area D4 is ordered to move to area C5 and attack the black soldier who resides there.* The order was plain and laconic, yet enough to bring darkness in his whole existence.

He did not want to go; this was an insane order that apparently had nothing to do with strategy and the *highest art of war*, it was just revenge to an expendable gay soldier with dreams that the others would never understand. He firmly decided to disobey; he was nobody's pawn. He did not have anything against the black soldier of C5, neither did he want to kill anybody else. If the King with his mad plans needed so much to win against the black king, who apparently was equally paranoiac, they could settle their disagreement on their own in something like a duel; even better, they could sort it out using some contest, for example a game of checkers; let them use the lifeless pawns of that board game, why should real soldiers kill each other?

Despite his determination, he had already put his small sack with all his things on his shoulders, grabbed his sword and shield and was on his way for C5. For God's sake, he was called Delta, D for his friends, he started this war at D2 and at some point, he came to D4, he had no business in the C regions! Nonetheless, he was still going; it was as if some invisible giant was literally holding him by his head and dragging him to C5.

"Stop right there!" the black soldier at C5 snarled as he saw a white soldier entering his territory.

Delta looked at him now that he was close and saw that they were not that different in the end, nor did he look savage or frightening; on the contrary, the black soldier looked scared like him. In reality, he did look like him in many ways. Sure, he was black and Delta was white, that was the major difference, but rather than that they looked the same, the colour was just one minor difference, a tiny *delta* they'd call it in maths, that could separate them. "I come in peace", he said confidently. He did follow the order to arrive there, but he would not do the same with the attacking part.

"I said stop and go back to D4! This is black army territory. If you make one more step, I will kill you", the black soldier tried to sound determined.

Delta was still moving forward thinking of ways to persuade him that he did not want to do any harm. "Listen to me", he said as calmly as he could, "we do not have to fight, you know. It is true, my King says so and I am sure yours does the same. But we are soldiers, it seems we were *born* soldiers, we have similar height and posture, we should stand together". Suddenly he had an epiphany: "And I suppose we have the same dreams, don't we? That one, that I am the Queen, I see it every time I fall asleep, sometimes more than once. I bet you have it too, don't you?"

The black soldier was now bemused. How on earth did this white soldier know about his dream? The vision that he had every night, sometimes more than once and it was torturing him and, while he did seek the opportunity to share it with someone, he never did? For a moment he believed the enemy soldier; they were one, they were united, they shared lives and dreams. However, then he remembered what he was told on the very first day of the war during his training and then it was repeated to him many times: "Attention! The white army has developed the nastiest techniques of psychological warfare. You should always be prepared for this". So that was it: psychological warfare; a trick to grab his attention and make him lower his defence, so that the sneaky enemy would grab the opportunity to take his life. He was furious now; he grabbed his sword firmly and he attacked against Delta.

For a moment, Delta had the feeling that the black soldier was believing him, so he did not expect the sudden frenzied attack. He did duck and avoided the attacker's sword and then, doing a move that he did not think of, instead it was rather a reflex, he stuck his sword into the black soldier's chest. The enemy fell into the ground.

"NOOOOOOO!" Delta made a glorious cry. He started shaking the dead body hoping it would come back to life; then he began weeping and talking incoherently, saying that he was sorry, he did not mean it and that he would fix this, because he was not a pawn. He was sitting there lamenting for some minutes, so he did not notice the black soldier who came from B6 and struck his back with his sword.

Delta had often thought about death and what (if anything at all) happens after. He had read several theories coming from religion, science, and philosophy and he could not decide which he believed; now that he actually did die, what happened was beyond his wildest imagination. He was in a place outside the battlefield; in reality, he found out that the entire world of the living was that miserable battlefield and, while he was not in that world anymore, he could see it in its totality now. In that new world that he was he found some other people who died in the war before him and he understood that they were sitting blacks and whites together, without being enemies, which made him very happy.

The black soldier who Delta had killed came and hugged him telling him that he did not need to say he is sorry, nothing was his fault. Even though they could clearly see the battlefield and all that was happening there, nobody really cared, they knew that that war and everything related to it was completely meaningless. It was a big feast! In reality, it was similar to what Delta imagined, but could not remember, as the state before the war.

Soon the Bishop also died, and he came embarrassed to find Delta and tell him that he was sorry, because he knew about his suicide mission in C5, but he could not do anything, in reality he was strictly following orders. Delta laughed and said that he did not care, the real life started now, it was the one *after the war*.

A bit later (though time in this afterlife was measured much differently than in the living world) the Queen also died. She fell bravely at the peak of the fight. This time Delta could not hold it anymore, he did wait a lifetime, now it was time to approach her.

"Hey!" he told her meaningfully.

"Oh, Delta!" she cried. "My favourite soldier! Oh, how safe I was at the start of the war having this brave and faithful guardian in front of me", she said, and she kissed him on the cheek. Delta's face became as red as a beetroot and he felt as if he had drunk at once a barrel of wine.

The most impressive piece of news that came from the field was a story about a black soldier who reached area F1 and he magically transformed into a queen! Everybody found this unbelievable, but for Delta for some reason it was not that surprising, he just felt happy for the fellow. A little before he went to sleep, he heard the news that the King also died, so the black army did win the war in the end. They said that the King came to find them and apologised for his actions, though he said that he was, in reality, also following orders, which he often wanted to disobey, but it was impossible. The king was also a pawn! In the past these would be colossal news for Delta, however, now they sounded so trivial and petty. He dozed into a happy sleep.

The soldier woke up. He had a bitter, stiff taste in his mouth, like the one you get when you have drunk a lot of low-quality wine the night before, yet he knew that there was no alcohol consumption involved in this case. He felt thirsty, in need of a glass of cool water, but for some reason he lit a cigarette instead. He had this strange dream once again; he would see it over and over almost every night, sometimes more than once. It was beautiful while it lasted, however it did leave this bitter taste in his mind when he was up. *Can one have a hangover because of a dream?* he wondered.

He was in area E2, this was the district he had to defend, and they made it clear that

26

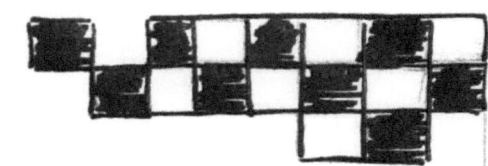

it was a position of absolute importance, since he was in front of the great King. On his back, diagonally with his left eye, he could take a quick glimpse of the Queen.

~ Georgios Dagkakis

27

Fish for lunch

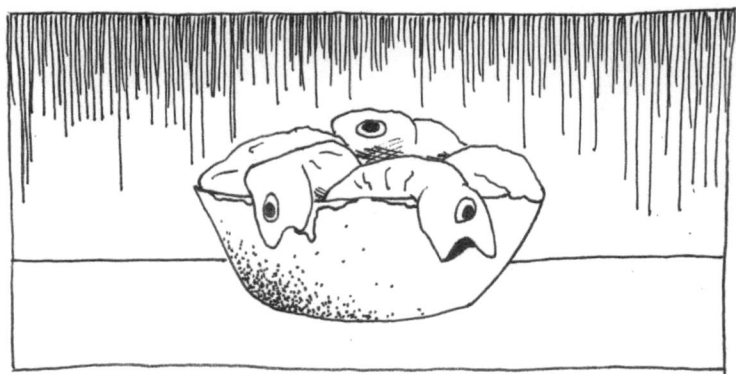

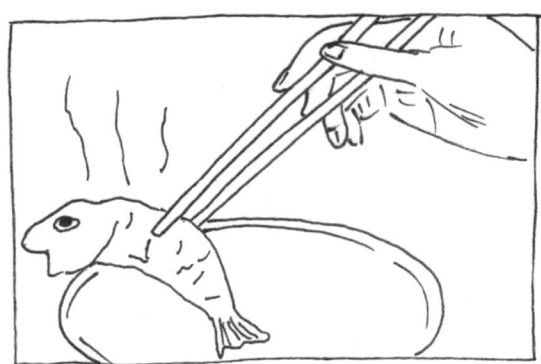

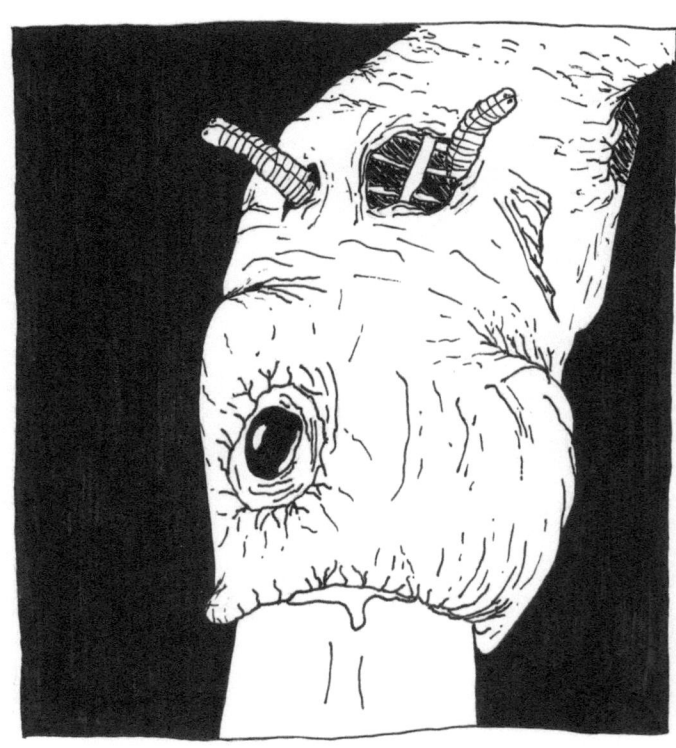

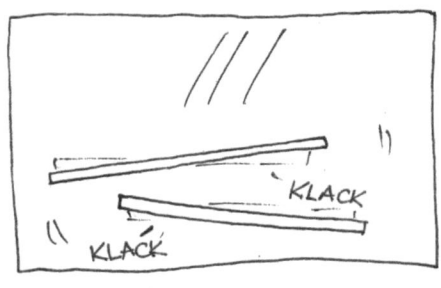

KLACK

KLACK

Rendez-vous

Today I plan to get a book from the bookcase
Whichever, I will pick randomly from some shelf
Only rule: it should be a book that you have read

I will sit on the sofa
Get lost in the pages, one after the other
I will have forgotten how all this started

Until I reach one of your marks
It can be an underlined paragraph
Maybe some word you circled with a colorful pen

A note on the margin, *see also Proust*
Sometimes a huge exclamation mark
Others three question marks next to each other

That's how I want to meet you today

~ *Georgios Dagkakis*

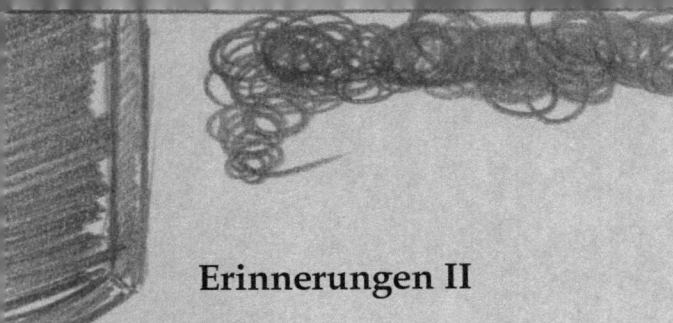

Erinnerungen II

17 Jahre sind vergangen.
Zum ersten Mal stehe ich hier an Helmuts Grab.

Zur Zeit seines Unfalls waren wir schon längst weggezogen.
Zur Beerdigung wollte man uns Kinder damals nicht fahren.
Wieder einmal hatte jemand ~~für uns~~ entschieden,
dass wir keinen Abschied nehmen,
dass wir so tun, als ließe die Person nur ein Leerzeichen zurück.
Denn gesprochen wurde über nichts ,
weder damals
noch heute, 20 Jahre später.

Wir stehen am Grab, erneuern die Blumen, machen Fotos
für die Familie,
damit sie sieht, dass die Floristin auch ihrer Arbeit nachgeht.
Ich habe meine Lieblingssüßigkeit mitgebracht und lege sie auf das Grab,
zusammen mit einem Brief, den ich an Helmut geschrieben habe,
den Helmut, an den ich mich erinnere.

Erinnerungen.
An Helmut hab ich nur wenige.

Er war viel unterwegs.
Und wenn er da war,
dann nur
kurz.
Oft pustete er mir in den Bauch, bis ich vor lauter Lachen nicht mehr atmen
konnte.
Dann ermahnte er noch meinen Bruder und meine anderen Cousins,
mich nicht zu ärgern.
Und schließlich
machte er sich wieder auf den Weg.

Ich habe mir jedes Mal gewünscht, dass er länger bleibt.

~ Chen-Rui

30

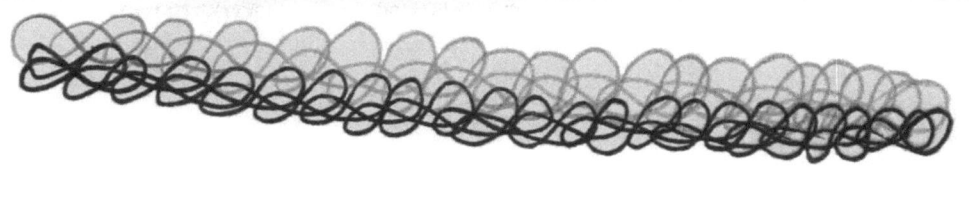

A unique gift

As Zeuxis was requested to paint beautiful Helen, he gathered five among the most beautiful daughters of Athens in order to collect from each of them her most precious feature.

> *Here an ear, a female deer*
>
> *There eyes, a water well*
>
> *A mouth of juicy fruits*
>
> *Further ahead hands, marmor pentelicum*
>
> *And from the last one curly hair made of myrrh*

When the storyteller was asked to write a story about you, he summoned the five dearest among your most beautiful memories.

> *Here soul*
>
> *There soul*
>
> *A little further on, soul*
>
> *Soul*
>
> *My soul*

Time went by and Zeuxis coincidentally encountered the storyteller as fellow traveler in Acheron, where they deposited the required fee in order to cross the river of *ach* and reach the Ithaca of eternity.

As the task was accomplished the empty boat returns back on Upper World carrying from both of them

a unique gift

A beautiful Soul

~ Stella Chachali

Addicts

Wir suchen den Rausch | so weit sind wir innerlich verfault.
Unsere Drogenkultur macht den Alltag erträglich
Es gibt Social Media, Alkohol, Koks, Serien, Zucker, Einkaufsbummeln und und und |
Damit lässt sich alles lösen.
Dopamin
Serotonin
Noradrenalin
...
Es <u>gibt</u> all dies nicht.

    Hab' voll Bock auf Keta, ist letztendlich mein Geburtstag, sagt eine.
    Die Verwesung wächst, Dorian!
       Cut. (Ein Cut ohne Rausch)

Du musst dich dem stellen, was dich in Panik versetzt.
Du siehst diese Bilder, die Finsternis, die Trübnis – du wirst sie schon längst verspürt
haben – du wirst sie kommen gesehen haben und trotzdem,
die Flucht wird leichter in Kauf zu nehmen gewesen sein.
du schmeckst, du riechst, du tastest die Gefahr, kommendes Chaos.
du spürst die Lebendigkeit deiner Sinne,
du denkst: ich muss fliehen!
Du musst geflohen sein! weggerannt, ohne Schuhe, sein!

du hörst den Fluss, ein Pumpen, schneller pumpen, nur pumpen.
du wirst deine Hände zu Fäusten geballt haben.
du wirst dich vor dir selbst gegruselt haben.
Du wirst gelebt haben, dich nicht berauscht haben, nicht gelähmt
haben.

Cut.

Ist das Entsetzen größer als der Wunsch zu leben?
Der Wille wird uns nicht vom Leiden befreien.

Es wird immer eine Frage der Stärke gewesen sein: ob man noch die
Kraft aufbringt, um weiterzukämpfen oder ob man sich
unterdrücken lässt.
Die eigenen Gedanken. Das innere Chaos. Die Ambiguität. Die
Verfolgung des Selbsthasses und der eigenen Finsternis. Wenn die
Brust drückt und der Atem stockt, wenn man in einem tiefen und
tieferen Loch versinkt.
Warum? fragt sich jede/r der Verfolgten. Warum muss ich damit
leben? Das wird nie die richtige Frage gewesen sein.

~ *Mirona C.*

Lines.

You wake up as the morning sunlight slips through the window and creeps across your room. Opening your eyes, you realise you didn't close the blinds before you passed out last night. At least you didn't pass out on the sofa this time.

You reach over to check your phone. 8:20am. You begin your morning ritual of scrolling semi-attentively through social media and news sites, not looking for or at anything in particular, deferring in your pre-caffeine lethargy the eventual effort of getting up and out of bed.

As you sit and scroll, you remember suddenly that Katie is still in your apartment. You left her alone in the living room before you went upstairs to pass out on your bed last night. For a long minute you consider going directly to her and beginning your day with her on the couch. You know she couldn't have moved, but something in you wants to check on her, reassure yourself she is still there.

You suddenly regret not having gotten rid of her yesterday evening.

Hey, Katie calls out to you, somehow sensing that you are awake. You don't respond.

Yesterday at work, you struggled to keep Katie out of your thoughts. Early in the day you told yourself that you would be strong that evening; that when you came home you would set boundaries, stay away from her, perhaps even get her out of the apartment. Making these promises to yourself helps you feel less pathetic.

You get up out of bed and head to the kitchen, passing Katie on your way, your eyes fixed straight ahead. She greets you as you move through the living room. *You have today off work, right?* She knows your entire schedule.
"Yeah," you reply. "But I still have plenty to do. We can't... we can't do anything together today." You make yourself a cup of coffee.
What do you have to do that's so important? Katie asks.
"I need to get this thesis chapter done," you answer. "I haven't answered my supervisor's emails in three weeks. He probably thinks I've vanished off the face of the earth. Or that I've dropped out of uni. Or something."
Okay, so you don't actually have to see anyone today. We could...
"No," you cut her off. "No. I'm sorry. I need to get this done."
Yeah, sure, Katie replies. *You said that yesterday, too.*
"I know," you answer. You have a nervous feeling you're going to spend all day together anyway, no matter how much you protest. As you begin to sip your coffee in the kitchen, you spend a moment thinking through how much work you need to get done today. You wonder briefly if you could get away with putting it off until tomorrow.

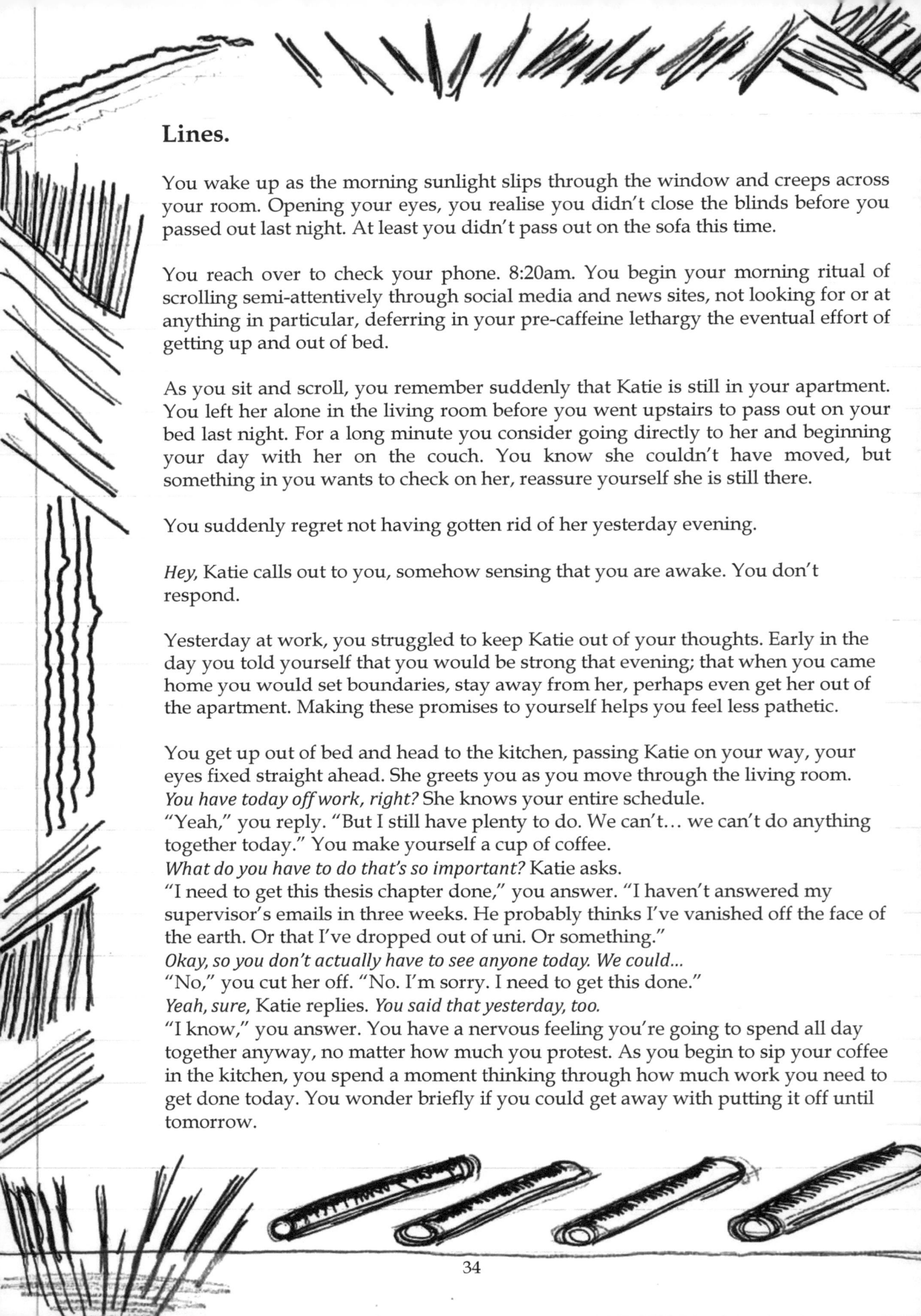

34

"No," you say aloud, suddenly.

Then kick me out of here, if you don't want me.

You don't answer. You could throw her out of your apartment right now. But you know you won't, just as you didn't yesterday, or the day before.

We could just spend the morning together. You'll be able to work afterwards.

"No, I won't," you answer.

But you'll be more relaxed then. She's right about that part.

"Yeah, but then I won't get any real work done. It'll be another day lost. I can't keep doing this."

Do you really think you're going to get any work done like this? Standing here and arguing with me all day?

"It'd be a lot easier if you'd just shut up and leave me alone for a while," you answer.

But you keep talking to me, too, Katie replies.

You skip breakfast and head directly to your desk. If you can just get into the flow of work now, you'll be able to concentrate. Katie calls out to you again as you sit down, but you ignore her. You open the document and start reading over the first half of the chapter you drafted on Wednesday. "Chapter 5: Research methodology." Your eyes scan line after line of what is perhaps the dullest chapter of your dissertation.

Hey. Katie returns after a few minutes. You hadn't been able to focus anyway.

It's a beautiful morning. We could lie in the sunlight, just you and me, on the sofa. You can forget about everything for a few good hours.

You feel your chest tightening.

You open a drawer next to your desk and look across at Katie. You heart begins to pound in your ribcage as you breath in and out slowly and imagine reaching out to her. You feel your hands clench into fists as you try to ignore the feeling in your stomach, in your chest, and turn back to your screen. You begin reading again.

You have a free day, Katie reminds you again. *Do you really want to waste this chance with me? No one else needs to know.*

A sense of loss washes over you, a grief at the thought of a lost opportunity to spend one more day together with Katie on your sofa, on your bed, on the floor.

"Just give me until the afternoon," you tell her.

So you'll spend the afternoon with me, then?

"I guess," you say, realising that you have just compromised with her. A sigh escapes your lips. Not even 9am and you are already compromising.

"Maybe," you add, hoping you might still be able to backtrack.

Not maybe, Katie answers with a laugh. *You know this is happening.*

Like a prize fighter, Katie watches you for the slightest opening, the slightest unguarded vulnerability to exploit. She knows your schedule as well as you do and scans it constantly for any window of time she can appropriate for herself.

An evening alone, a day off from work, a weekend by yourself while your girlfriend is out of town. You let her do this. So far she hasn't cost you your job, or your scholarship, or your girlfriend. You tell yourself you can still manage this relationship. You just need to get better at setting boundaries. You told yourself that yesterday, and the day before.

You shake your head, trying to snap out of it.
"Not now. Not this morning," you insist. "I'm getting this chapter done. I told Paul I'd have it finished by last Friday."

The next hour proceeds much like the last. Now and again you stand, pace around the living room, before sitting back down at your desk. Compromising with Katie about spending the afternoon together has opened a crack in door that you should have kept closed. Why wait until the afternoon?, you find yourself asking, as Katie mockingly eggs you on. You *could* spend all day together, lying on the couch in an dissociative embrace, just her sweet touch and breath mixing with yours. You want her. If you had nothing else to do today, you'd be all over her. You sit there and remind yourself of how important this scholarship is to you, what consequences will await you if you allow Katie to come between you and your dissertation day after day.

Katie beckons again, not relenting. *Do you really want to waste this chance?*
You suddenly realise that you won't have another chance with Katie for at least three more days. Tomorrow you'll be visiting your girlfriend, heading out of town. It could be days until you can be with Katie again. A sense of loss, almost grief, washes over you. You sense the tension in your chest grow tighter, constricting.
Can you last that long without me?

The world is still for a numb minute. You open the drawer next to your desk again and stare at Katie. You look at her tiny white crystals, whiter than snow, glistening through the clear plastic bag she sits in. The tightness in your chest drops to your stomach, where it claws at you, a singular animal desire. An urge rises in you: to grab Katie right there, spread her out upon the table, cut her into two thick lines and take her into yourself. You can already smell her strange, chemical scent; you taste her cleaving to the back of your throat, your world collapsing into her numb embrace, the darkness of her oblivion. You want her. More than you care about your dissertation, more than you want to succeed at anything, or impress anyone, or get anywhere in life, you want her. You feel your willpower fading, but you don't care anymore. Fuck the afternoon. You can be together now.

36

Suddenly your phone vibrates. The screen lights up with a message notification. You reach over and see that it's from Daniel.

hey bro
hey, you answer.
is katie at ur place?

Daniel still feigns discretion, using the same codeword you've had for years. You've told him at least five times that you're not a dealer, but he still messages you whenever he runs out and his usual guy in town isn't answering.

You stare at his message on your backlit screen. You're down to your last half gram, not enough to share. You contemplate the possibility of Daniel taking Katie from you. A flicker of courage rises somewhere inside of you. The animal clawing its way through your gut and tightening your chest roars in defiance.
Do you really want him to ruin this for us? Katie snaps, realising that she is threatened. *We won't have another chance for days. Don't let him come here. This is our day. You wanted this. Don't.*

yeah she's here. You type and hit Send.

Daniel wastes no time in replying:
can I come pick her up? I'm nearby
yeah. come over now.
ok, see u soon

You sit there, not moving, for a long minute. Daniel is on his way, probably with cash, to take Katie off your hands. You feel the tightness in your chest begin to fade, and with it the urge that had clawed at your insides just moments earlier. You turn back to your dissertation. Katie falls silent, interrupted and betrayed.

He's disappointed you only have half a gram, but takes it, dropping a fifty dollar note on the table. You tell him to keep it.
"What?"
"Keep it. I told you, I'm not a dealer."
Daniel looks at you quizzically.
"I was going to throw it out anyway. I need to cut down. Just take it."
Daniel picks up the note from table, his expression still sceptical.
"You sure, man?"
"Yeah, just take it."
"Alright," he says with a grin. "What's the plan for today?"
"I'm finishing off a chapter for my thesis," you tell him. "I actually need to be getting back to it." You tell him something about how you keep getting distracted,

about how you haven't responded to your supervisor, about how the work has piled up on you for weeks now and you keep ruining every chance you get to work on it.

"Alright, man, I'll leave you to it" Daniel says, standing to leave. "Just try turning your phone off. Works for me. Fucking smartphones, man. We're bloody addicted to them these days. Can't get anything done." You don't reply. You watch Daniel slip Katie into his jacket pocket.

You say your goodbyes and Daniel leaves.

You head back over to the desk, sit down in front of your laptop, and return to the driest chapter of your thesis. Katie leaving the apartment has closed a door within you.

You know she will be back; sometime next week you will call around until you find her and wind up, again, dissolved in her numb oblivion on your couch, her chemical taste clinging to the back of your throat while you float away into another universe. But for now, for today, for this weekend she is gone, as is the tightness in your chest. Concentration comes quickly as you get back to work.

~ Tim Redfern

ECHOLOT

Erst im Dialog, in der Korrespondenz findet Zaraffel seinen Sinn:

Wurde ein Zaraffel von einer Kritzelei berührt, so hat er hier die Möglichkeit, dieser Stimme zu antworten, einen Ruf abzusetzen und das, was ihm vorgegeben wurde, in eigener Stimme zu interpretieren.

Als experimentellster Teil des Magazins bildet unser Echolot spontane kreative Prozesse ab und fügt dem Referenztext auf diese Weise eine Facette hinzu, vervollständigt ihn so, wie es im bloßen Gespräch nicht möglich wäre.

Auf welchen Text jeweils Replik genommen wird, erkennt ihr am verwendeten Rahmen.

Dabei kann es auch vorkommen, dass ein Echo auf einen Text aus vergangenen Ausgaben Bezug nimmt, haltet also Ausschau!

Encounters, missed and marginal.

I was 17 when I first met H among a group of friends one afternoon. I can't remember who brought her along, but we clicked quickly. We spent the following weeks chatting every night after school, still using MSN on our PCs in the final months of the pre-smartphone era. As an awkward kid without much to say, it wasn't often that I experienced that level of attention.

After a few weeks we were talking one day about books. She asked me to recommend her something, and I told her I would bring her a novel the next time we saw each other. I knew immediately what to give her: my orange Penguin Classics edition of Jack London's *The Call of the Wild*.

I suppose it's a weird novel to give to a girl you like when you're 17, but in retrospect I realise why I identified with it. Raging against the environment of a conservative Australian private school, Jack London was revolutionary with his energetic announcements of a life force beyond civilization and bourgeois aspirations.

On the night before I gave the book to H, I spent hours highlighting, underlining and annotating my favourite passages. I searched for those passages where London praised the highest peaks of experience and the ecstasies of self-forgetting, where he evoked the primordial womb of Time and the tidal wave of being. These I underlined, ensuring H would see them, read them again and again, understand that they mattered. I scrawled my exclamation marks next to London's prose, highlighting here, underling there. I worshipped the power of his words to push the liminal boundaries of experience. The transcendental of the raw, the ecstatic, the power of Being; that was what I wanted to share.

She smiled as I gave her the book the next day, promising to read it.

After handing it to her, for weeks I oscillated between nervous anticipation and regret at having exposed a part of myself in those margins of paper. Within a few weeks, however, it was all over. H and I had a falling out and stopped talking.

She returned my annotated orange Penguin Classic via a mutual friend about a month later.
"She never read it," he said.

I was 27 when, on a hot summer day wandering between corrugated iron laneways and tram tracks, I discovered a small, second-hand esoteric bookstore hidden away up a staircase leading off Sydney Road. In one room they had shelves of books on alternative medicine; another room was devoted to books on Buddhism and Indian religions, another to global poetry and literature, and another to philosophy, mysticism and world religions. It was as if half the store had been curated just for me and my fringe interests.

In one and a half honours I bought more books there than I ever did at any other bookstore. I lugged home a heavy cardboard box of second-hand volumes: a few books on Zen, the sermons of Meister Eckhart, an introduction to Sufi hermeneutics, Guénon and Huxley on the perennial philosophy, and perhaps a dozen others.

Arriving home, I began to skim through them, still in awe at my luck. I realised quickly that most of the books in this eclectic collection had a few things in common. The same delicate handwriting, in gentle graphite pencil, had annotated almost all of them. On the inside covers someone had written indexes, lists of themes and key passages with page numbers for easy reference. With a ruler this same hand had carefully underlined the most beautiful passages and most memorable quotes, while lines in pencil linked ideas and quotes across paragraphs and pages.

Who had owned this library before I found it? Whoever it was, they were a kindred spirit.

I know my interests are odd. I have long ago accepted this isolation. But in the pages of those dozen books, in the same graphite pencil handwriting, I met a soulmate, a mind who loved the same things I do, who was moved by the same ideas that could stir excitement within me. In those annotated margins, they showed me connections that my eyes would have missed, asked questions that would leave me wondering for days.

I had been getting to know this person for months by the time I stumbled on a slip of paper they left in one book, a neatly written note hidden between the pages of an aged paperback. It was the first time I had noticed it.

It read,

"Was reading The Practice of Zen by Garma C. C. Chang in the afternoon on the tram. Read a passage that describes an experience of Void by Zen Master Han Shan, which had the effect of giving me a temporary taste of that State. I sat still and realised I had no body or mind. All I could see was one great illuminating Whole-omnipresent, perfect, lucid and serene. All images and shadows had dropped away into the all tranquil-Voidness. It had the effect of freeing me from anxiety and self-concerns. It was as if the doors of perception were rolled back."

As I read this note, I realised that my connection with this strange new friend of mine had reached a new dimension. I had to find them.

I went to the bookstore on Sydney Road, taking with me a few volumes that were marked with the same neat handwriting. I told the bookseller that I needed to know where these books came from, who they belonged to. Do they live nearby? Is it someone who comes here often? I imagined this friend of mine as a regular, coming every few months to pick up a new haul of books and drop off another box of annotated, pre-loved volumes. I had to meet this person who I had gotten to know so intimately, who had shared so much with me already. There was so much I had to learn from them, so many questions, so many hours and hours of conversations to be had.

"He's dead," the woman behind the counter told me. "When he died, his wife dropped off all his books here. Some of them are rare classics."

Of course, I said. Rare classics indeed.

~ *Tim Redfern*

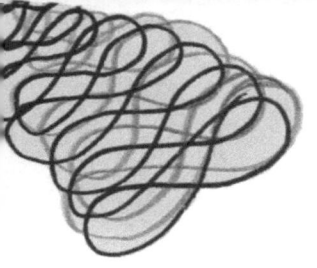
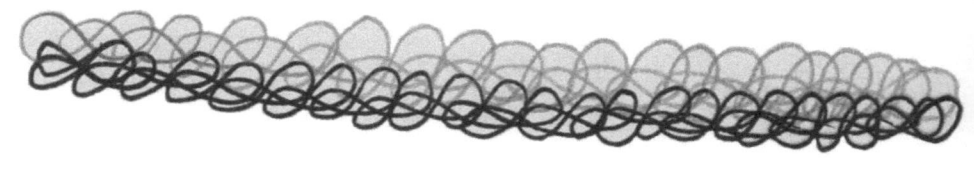

Eucharist

Later, the musician was requested to dress life with a tune and he collected the most beautiful sounds that he could find in his universe

Sssh! Listen, far away a waterfall
Above in the sky a mocking bird sings
The wind whistles among the leaves of a tree
Suddenly, a thunderbolt
Nativity, a baby is laughing

Yet he remained silent, he was afraid of challenging the gods - who can forget the fate of Marcyas?
When he died he played his tune to the ferryman and for an instant Acheron became as colourful as Venice during carnival.
Charon was pleased with this new Orpheus; he could not bring him back to the living, but he promised to carry his song for the sake of Life.
Just before his passenger disembarked to the Underworld, he shared with him a secret:

One picture is worth a thousand words, they say
One melody is worth a thousand pictures
But in the end, the Word is God

~ Georgios Dagkakis

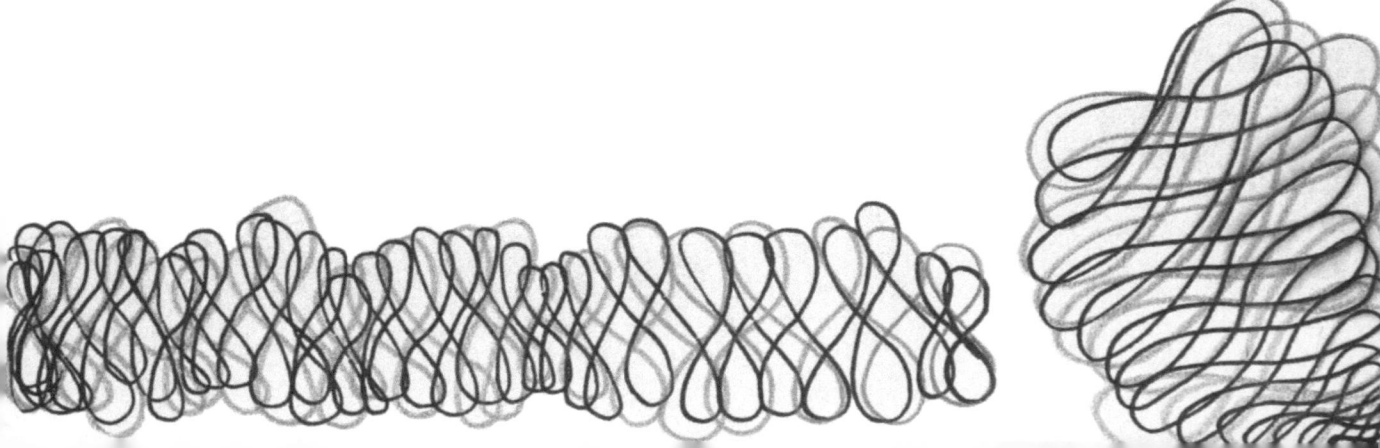

_____ (Titel einfügen)

Ich kaufe, du kaufst, er/sie/es kauft, wir kaufen, ihr kauft, sie kaufen;
Ich esse, du isst, er/sie/es isst, wir essen, ihr esst, sie essen;
und schneller!
Ich kaufe, du kaufst, er/sie/es kauft, wir kaufen, ihr kauft, sie nehmen;
Ich fresse, du frisst, er/sie/es frisst, wir fressen, ihr fresst, sie tanzen;
lauter!
ICH GIERE, DU GIERST, ER/SIE/ES GIERT, WIR GIEREN, IHR GIERT, SIE RAFFEN;
ICH ERSTICKE, DU ERSTICKST, ER/SIE/ES ERSTICKT, WIR ERSTICKEN, IHR ERSTICKT, SIE LACHEN;
leise
Ich zweifle, du zweifelst, zweifelst du?, er/sie/es zweifelt;
Ich glaube, du glaubst, er/sie/es glaubt – woran?;
Ich frage mich, ich frage dich, ich frage ihn, ich frage sie, ich frage euch: Wo ist das „wir"?;
Ich renne, du rennst, er/sie/es rennt, wir rennen, ihr rennt, sie rennen – wohin?;
Ich kann nicht, ich kann nicht, ich kann nicht, ich kann nicht;
Ich will nicht, ich will nicht, ich will nicht, ich will nicht;
STOPP |
Ich atme… du atmest … er/sie/es atmet… wir atmen… ihr atmet… sie atmen…
zusammen
Ich leide, du leidest, er/sie/es leidet, wir leiden;
Ich entscheide, du entscheidest, er/sie/es entscheidet, wir entscheiden;
Ich lebe, du lebst, er/sie/es lebt, wir leben.

~ *Chen-Rui*

43

Pool of words

Es wird wärmer

Freischwimmer

Bangigkeit = κατάσταση αγωνίας

Kindisch dekadente
  Prokrastinationsausbrüche

Unterrichtsstunde

Zuträglichkeit = ωφελιμότητα

Improvisieren

Freischwimmen

Hitzefrei = άδεια λόγω καύσωνα

Schule

Gefängnis

Gesetzesfreie Zone

YoutubeVideos

Mousse au chocolat

Das pädagogische Highlight

Feriengefühle

Sanduhr

Das Spiel ist ausgespielt

Publikumsränge wieder leer

Erinnerungen

Selbstermächtigung

Escolios oder ein Liebesbrief

Words are born among the people,
Flourish among writers,
And die in the mouth of the middle class.

Gómez Dávila

Allein in der Klasse

ein Tier, das gefüttert werden soll

oder eine Pflanze, die darauf wartet

gegossen zu werden.

Corps sans Organes

voll von Flüssigkeiten:

Verzweiflung

Bangigkeit

YoutubeVideos

Ich bin 10+3 Jahre alt

Geschlecht: unentschieden

Selbstbewusstsein: nebelhaft

Erinnerungen: noch einzuschreiben

Ein *Freischwimmer* steht auf der *Bühne*

Die Tafel noch unbeschrieben

Das hidden curriculum ein desiteratum

verschoben vom *Hitzefrei*.

Es wird wärmer.

Liegend auf dem leeren Boden meiner
Innerlichkeit

Ich höre ihm zu

Komische Wörter entfliehen
seinem Mund,

exotische Vögel

in einer gesetzesfreien Zone.

Die *Unterrichtsstunde* vorbereitet

wie ein perfekt gemachtes Bett vor dem
Schlafengehen

Plötzlich versucht er

freizuschwimmen.

Die *Zuträglichkeit* löst sich auf.

Der Sandmann wirft die *Sanduhr* in mein
Auge.

Selbstermächtigung: schiefgelaufen

Ich leihe seine Wörter von anderen Seiten aus.

Ich quäle sie mit zärtlicher Brutalität

Ihr Sinn ist verloren und trotzdem

spüre ich ihr indecent proposal.

Seine Wörter fliegen im Klassenzimmer

wie Papierflugzeuge.

Ich bin getroffen. Bingo.

Anfang der *Sommerferien.*

Das Spiel ist ausgespielt.

„Du musst mit Kindern gleichen Alters
spielen"

Ich stoße mich am Bildschirm

und spiele nur mit den Fingern.

Ich bin in Wörter verliebt.

Platonische Liebe oder

List des Odysseus?

Ich zeige ihm den Vogel durch das Fenster

Letztendlich bin ich nur ein Kind,

das wild auf *mousse au chocolat* ist.

~ *Stella Chachali*

Träume I

Prolog

Hinter Gitterstäben stand vielleicht geschrieben, was lang vorher schon entwischt war. Weil mir das gerade wieder einfiel, begab ich mich auf Entdeckung nach noch mehr Erinnerung. Man muss nur die Ruhe behalten und viel Geduld. Ich öffnete die Schubladen, tauchte mich hinein, ließ akribisch keinen Zettel unberührt, keine Formel ungewendet, doch nichts. Eilige Fächer schleiften aneinander, Unsortiertes lag erst überall verteilt, wuchs zu Haufen und ganze Stapel von Unterlagen galt es bald wieder umzuwälzen; um nachträglich mehr Platz zu schaffen standen selbst Sitzgelegenheiten ineinander verschränkt als stumme Zeugen am Rand meiner Papierwelt. Allein, der Ansporn wird von fortdauernder Enttäuschung nicht satt.

Derweil stundete das Surren hinter der Röhre in die Schrankwand hinein, ließ den Abend in Nacht versinken. Leises Rauschen und ein Flackern, nur, war alles, was diese Schatzsuche noch beleuchtete. Aus einem spitzen Winkel endlich schimmerte es mir zu, dämmrig fahl wie es war, vielleicht bloße Einbildung, doch manchmal hat man Glück damit, und ich hatte es. So stieg ich auf einen Turm aus Stühlen und fand dich erneut, verstaubt, auf einem alten Regal zwischen Brettspielen meiner Jugend; ein dünnes Heft, nein, eigentlich bloß ein Karoblock, und trotzdem aus einem Traum gestohlen. Fünfzehn Zeilen auf des toten Mann Kiste.

Es war zeitig dunkel geworden, im Winter ist das normal. Unter dem viel zu warmen Licht der Schreibtischlampe wird der Blick schneller müde. Ein schmaler Finger fährt die Gitter in fünfzehn mal zwanzig Zentimetern entlang. Die Schrift, mal mit Tinte, mal mit Bleistift, mal mit was anderem, was eben gerade in der Nähe lag, doch immer mit eiliger Hand in dünnen blauen Strichen aufs Papier gebracht – war es blau oder grau? –, war so genau nicht auszumachen. Aus dem Hintergrund taucht das Rauschen auf, für einen Augenblick tritt es an die Oberfläche und versinkt sogleich in matten Zweifeln. Beim besten Willen, es war ununterscheidbar. Bleistifte schreiben nicht blau, hört man sich sagen, das gibt es nicht, aber dann erinnerte ich wieder, dass es bereits dunkel war und du weißt ja, was man sich sagt: dass nachts eben alle Katzen grau sind.

Das Piratenschiff war aus seinem Logbuch herausgeschnitten worden. Offenbar hatte es schnell gehen müssen. Manche Stellen sind gar keine echte Schrift; sind kaum mehr als eine sehr schmale Wellenlinie oder der zittrige Strich dieses einen Schülers, der versucht, freihändig ein gleichseitiges Dreieck zu zeichnen, weil sein Lineal längst zerbrochen im Ranzen knirscht, wenn man die Mappen und Bücher hinterherwirft (sollte er sie dabeihaben). Die Finger blättern weiter und die Seiten rascheln aneinander. Sie sind noch immer weich, fast sanfte Wogen; wenn man sich darauf einlässt, wird man auf ihnen fortgetragen. Dann schifft man sich ein, auf seinem Papierkreuzer. Kreuz und quer gehen die Wellen und auf ihnen der Blick, erst hin und her, dann auf und ab, anschließend Wellenrauschen und der Rest war mir entwischt…

Hook

Als ich aufwachte, wehte noch der letzte Satz in meinem Kopf, den ich geträumt haben musste. Man hatte ihn mir aus dem Nichts hinterhergerufen – –. Ein hektischer Moment, der meinen Puls beim Erwachen auf Vollmast brachte: „Gib acht, Jolly Roger wird verschwunden sein, bei Nacht!" Langsam tauchte das Rauschen aus dem Hintergrund auf. Es regnete. Sanfte Tropfen klopften an Fensterscheiben, die ich zuerst nicht als mir unbekannt erkannte, aber so ist das jedes Mal, kurz nachdem man in einem fremden Haus erwacht. Von draußen schlich dunkles Licht am Fenster vorbei, wurde durch die kleinen Linsen an der Fensterscheibe zerstreut und ich sah ihre Interpretation an der gegenüberliegenden Wand des Zimmers abgebildet. Ein kurzer Film spielte sich dann ab, wobei zunächst das Abbild des Fensters von einer Seite der Wand zur nächsten getragen wurde, dann seinen Schatten schmälerte, bis er die Bühne wieder verließ und in Nacht unterging. Dieses Schauspiel, das jedes Kind kennt, dessen Zimmerfenster zur Straße hinzeigt, beruhigte die Nerven wieder. Schweiß auf meiner Stirn, brausende Brandung im Kopf war bald beruhigt in der rhythmischen Wiederkehr jenes Leuchtfeuers, das mich zu suchen schien. Doch weil außer ertränkten Regentropfen nichts zu hören war, konnte das Licht nicht von den gewohnten Autos stammen. Also entdeckte ich mich, glitt aus dem Bett, fand den Weg zur Zimmertür im Echolot des Pharos erneut und sah vom Türrahmen aus, dass auch ihr hier wart, unten im Haus, denn noch befand ich mich in der ersten Etage. Der Lichtschalter im Flur funktionierte nicht und spontan dachte ich an den Sturm, der für den Stromausfall verantwortlich gewesen sein könnte, verwarf den schlaftrunkenen Gedanken jedoch, da sich doch Licht von unten hinaufstohl.

Mit jedem Schritt nach unten, traten eure Stimmen sanfter aus menschlichem Lärm hervor. Bald begrüßte man mich und als ich mich umsah, begriff ich auch schon, dass ich der Letzte unter uns gewesen sein musste, der noch geschlafen hatte. Niemand hatte einen Zweifel, dass wir uns hier verabredet hatten, obwohl sich keiner mehr an die Besitzer des Hauses erinnerte. Wir waren jetzt vollzählig und konnten damit beginnen, unser Vorhaben in die Tat umzusetzen, unser Vorhaben, das so sehr wichtig gewesen ist, weil es unseren… Plan – da war es wieder!, das Licht, das von draußen hereinschien – langsam, in kreisrunder Bewegung, tasteten seine Finger lautlos am Haus entlang. Von hier unten konnte man es besser beobachten und es war klar, dass niemand auf diese Weise ein Auto fährt, zumindest kein Mensch. Gefolgt von euch, trat ich nach draußen und fand zunächst nur strömenden Regen, doch musste nicht lange warten, bis der Schatten der Westseite des Hauses in geometrischer Vollendung in blendendes Licht gestürzt wurde, gerade als er dabei war, einen überstumpfen Winkel zu zeichnen. Langsam, noch ganz langsam, entwöhnten sich meine der Dunkelheit angetrauten Augen, bis sie die Holzdielen der Veranda, die wandernden Schatten deren hölzernen Ständer, die blitzenden Schienen und schließlich die Quelle meiner Sprachlosigkeit lesen konnten.

Für einen Moment war da ein schwarzer Fleck, vom Tintenfass an die Wand zu werfen, der jedes Buch der Welt durchsickern würde, jede Erinnerung tilgen und alle Niedertracht vertuschen. Eine solche Welle durchflutete die Nacht, aber es dauerte, wie gesagt, nur einen Augenblick, bis das Unheil wieder um die Ecke des Herrenhauses geebbt war, und mit ihm der Druck in meinem Herzen sank. Noch ehe ich mir gewahr werden konnte, um was es sich handelte, noch ehe ich mich hätte umdrehen können, um euch danach zu fragen, wuchsen die Schatten zu meiner Linken von neuem, wuchsen rasch, zeichneten verzerrte Grimassen aus ehemals gewohnten Mustern, stiegen aus der Nacht, schmissen sich in die Tiefe hinab; mit verzogenem Knarzen und dampfendem Groll, zuletzt, erloschen alle Bewegungen jenes Irrlichts direkt zu meinen Füßen, von dem kurz zuvor ich mich noch bereitwillig hätte fortführen lassen.

Plötzlich dämmerte mir, dass das ganze Haus eigentlich ein Karussell übertriebenen Ausmaßes war, auf dessen innerer, unbeweglichen Plattform wir uns befanden und dem Treiben des einzigen Gefährts, welches darum sich immerfort zu drehen schien, zuschauten. In der Tat, um das gesamte Anwesen und fest mit ihm verbaut, kreiste ein Segelschiff: Die Hook. Offenbar handelte es sich um eine detailgetreue Miniatur des Originals aus Nimmerland, die uns von Steuerbord aus einlud. Auf den zweiten Blick schien alles fachmännisch ausgeleuchtet und täuschend echt nachgebildet zu sein. Mein Verdacht war denn auch, wer mit diesem Schiff fahre, dürfe keinen einzigen Tag altern. Im Angesicht des Sturms, bisher und immerzu im Kreis, fuhr das Piratenschiff auch ohne seinen Kapitän. Vielleicht sprangen wir auf, als das Karussell allmählich wieder Fahrt aufnahm.

An Bord fand ich niemanden, die Besatzung musste das Schiff aufgegeben haben, so dachte ich; den Jolly Roger hatten sie vermutlich ebenfalls mitgenommen, denn der Fahnenmast ließ die Totenkopfflagge vermissen. Auf der Suche nach irgendwelchen Überbleibseln, wenigstens einem Schnipsel, durchsuchte ich die Kabinen, arbeitete mich von der Reling des Bugs nach Achtern durch, bis ich die Kapitänskajüte betrat, in der als einzigem Ort Stille herrschte. Im ersten Moment dröhnte die Abwesenheit des sonst so durchdringenden Prasselns lauter nach, als der Regen es je vermochte. Hier fand ich mich problemlos zurecht, ging auf und ab, hin und her, genoss dabei, wie der bordeauxfarbene Teppich den Klang meiner Schritte dämpfte, bis meine Finger am Schreibtisch entlangstreiften und ich mich setzte, um für kurze Zeit das aufwändig geschmückte Interieur in Gänze zu bestaunen. So entzündete ich eine Kerze, unter welcher sogleich ein mit dunkelblauer Tinte unterzeichnetes Stück Pergament hervorlugte. In feierlichen Serifen gestaltet, titelte das Dokument bloß „Vertrag" und als ich mich darüber beugte, um zu lesen was darauf stand, fiel mir auf, dass ich meine Brille oben im Schlafzimmer hatte liegen lassen und es damit aussichtslos war zu erkennen, um was es sich hierbei genau handelte.

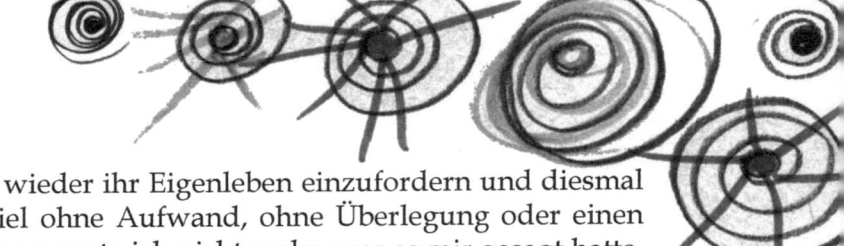

Und so begannen meine Hände wieder ihr Eigenleben einzufordern und diesmal fanden sie ihr ahnungsvolles Ziel ohne Aufwand, ohne Überlegung oder einen absurden Plan zu verfolgen. Zwar wusste ich nicht mehr, wer es mir gesagt hatte, doch ich erinnerte mich, dass die zweite Schublade von oben doppelbödig sein musste. Nach einigen kurzen Handgriffen schon bot mir das Fach sein Geheimnis preis: des Kapitän Logbuch. Zunächst ziellos, blätterte ich darin im Gedanken, man solle besser nicht zu tief in fremden Träumen tauchen, wo doch unversehrtes Erwachen nie restlos gesichert ist.

Die Handschrift im Logbuch hingegen war auch noch unter dem Flackern des Kerzenlichts ausreichend erkennbar. Ich riet mir, nur an einigen Stellen bruchstückhaft zu lesen, um so mein nervöses Herz zu beruhigen und trotzdem meiner Neugier dienlich zu bleiben.

Was ist merkwürdiger als Texte zu lesen, die man schon gekannt hat, obwohl das ganz unmöglich ist? Was sind Träume, wenn nicht fremde Erinnerungen? Als wüsste man, welche Schlussfolgerung auf die dritte ~~Welle~~ Prämisse folgte, noch bevor man den ersten Satz beendet hatte. An einer Stelle bestätigt der Autor mir sogar, was ich vermutete, nämlich dass weder Körper noch Geist an Bord der Hook altern könnten. Er versichert mir ausdrücklich, unterstreicht flutenartig, dass es **wahr** sei und warnt im Nachsatz sogleich: „Was du wolltest war die Finsternis zuzudecken? Gib acht, denn Jolly Roger wird verschwunden sein, bei Nacht. Die ganze Mannschaft wird dafür bezahlt haben, und zwar mit Haut und Haar. Und auch du bist nicht sicher, kleiner Narr!, denn jede Erinnerung an …"

…Hier ging es nicht weiter. Jemand hatte ein kleines Papierschiff aus dem Buch herausgeschnitten, ausgerechnet an dieser Stelle. Wer? Stummen Hohnes klaffte dieses Loch da einfach so im Bauch meiner Neugier und die Stille in der Kajüte lachte lauthals in sich hinein. Alles hier schien zu wissen, was vor sich ging, nur mir entfielen jegliche Begriffe. Mit zerschlagener Geste warf ich das Logbuch auf den Tisch, unfassbar weit entfernt, nahm es aber gleich wieder zur Hand, blätterte darin, drehte es auf den Kopf und schüttelte, dass es sein Rätsel auflöse, doch nichts. Das Papierschiff, wo konnte es hingekommen sein? Ich beschloss, mich auf die Suche danach zu machen, nahm das Logbuch an mich, vermerkte auf der nächsten leeren Seite ausführlich alles, was mir heute zugestoßen war. Anschließend las ich es noch einmal zur Korrektur, dann ein zweites Mal, sorgfältiger als sonst, so lange bis mich die Wellenlinien ans nächste Ufer trieben.

– – *Fortsetzung folgt* – –

~ Eising

Re/ written line

„...you remember suddenly that Katie is still in your apartment. [...] You suddenly regret not having gotten rid of her yesterday evening. "

My relationship with Katie was a special one. She knew my entire schedule. She would show up unexpectedly on my doorstep and demand that I let her in. For a while, at the beginning, I tried to get rid of her, but it never really worked. She knew all my soft spots (all the senses). Thus, I could throw objects at her, offensive words, try to dispose of her or
be a brute.
She would wait patiently for me to calm down, then seduce me or come back, whenever I was free. In short, Katie was my stalker.
I could never make a move, without her having knowledge of it. Sometimes she'd even snoop around my apartment, when I wasn't there. Was I terrified? More astonished at her grotesque courage. I didn't and did perceive her as an invader.

She'd convinced me once that we were meant for each other for I needed to cheat and she needed to be a mistress.
Spice things up. She called it.
She was right, one could have probably called me an addicted cheater. I was cheating not merely on my girlfriend, but on my friends and my professor and my own life in general. The thrill of feeling relentless, whenever I met her, would keep me going. I despised her for it and myself at times. And yet I was caught in this cobweb of secrecy, my analogous personality, the dimension of her.
Of course, it was poisonous; I risked losing everything each time I opened that door, that I would have rather kept shut and yet desperately craved to open. I realised how obnoxious this made me - something torturing and, by extension, voluptuous.
Katie could seduce me anytime she wanted. Her physicality. It was probably not even her, but me, (almost) expecting it of her – as if there was a contract between us. She wasn't attractive though, not to me.

We would spend entire naked days in my apartment. Was it like running, fleeing? more like a vicious sphere we'd created. Considering the rest of my everyday…
Black lace. Bare skin. Hedonism.
Sometimes I wondered how I would resist another day without that. Not her.
In short, Katie was my possession.

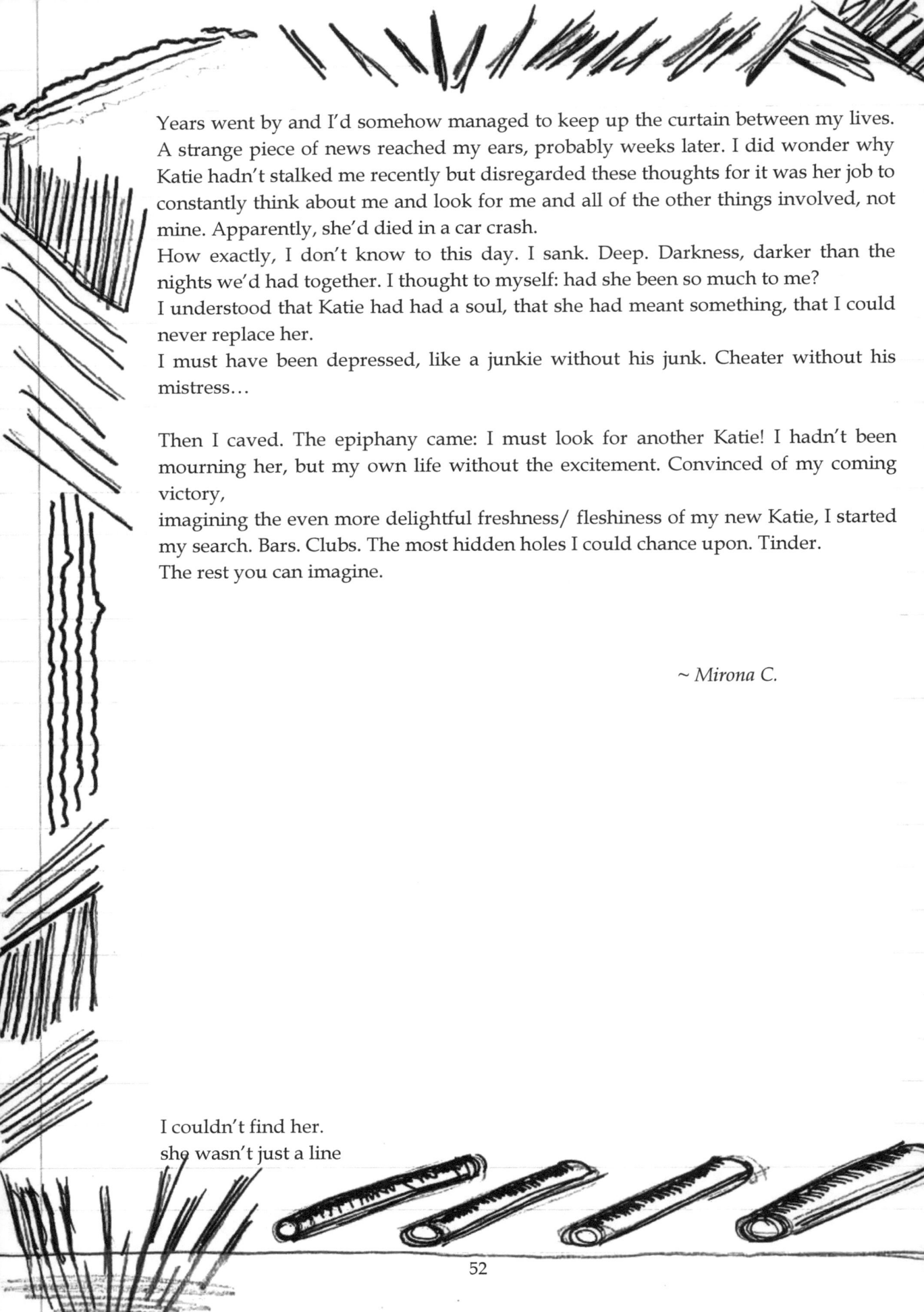

Years went by and I'd somehow managed to keep up the curtain between my lives. A strange piece of news reached my ears, probably weeks later. I did wonder why Katie hadn't stalked me recently but disregarded these thoughts for it was her job to constantly think about me and look for me and all of the other things involved, not mine. Apparently, she'd died in a car crash.

How exactly, I don't know to this day. I sank. Deep. Darkness, darker than the nights we'd had together. I thought to myself: had she been so much to me?

I understood that Katie had had a soul, that she had meant something, that I could never replace her.

I must have been depressed, like a junkie without his junk. Cheater without his mistress…

Then I caved. The epiphany came: I must look for another Katie! I hadn't been mourning her, but my own life without the excitement. Convinced of my coming victory,

imagining the even more delightful freshness/ fleshiness of my new Katie, I started my search. Bars. Clubs. The most hidden holes I could chance upon. Tinder.

The rest you can imagine.

~ Mirona C.

I couldn't find her.
she wasn't just a line

52

Taubenschlag

In jeder Ausgabe drucken wir hier Texte von euch ab.

Heute freuen wir uns euch unsere Gastautorin
Rika Sakalak
zu präsentieren.

Ein offener, spielerischer Umgang mit Texten sei ihr Anliegen, teilte sie uns mit. Vielfältige Zugänge zum Stoff zu entwickeln, ist ein den Lesenden zugewandtes Anliegen, das sich auch im Thema ihrer experimentellen Erzählung widerspiegelt.

Körper und Wasser spielen ihre Rollen auf verschiedensten Ebenen des Textes, gehen ineinander über, sowohl optisch als auch stilistisch. Die in dieser Grundidee ruhenden Assoziationspunkte verketten sich zu freier Interpretation.

Die Wordseite öffnet sich; weiß und blau. / Take your marks

Das Wasser berührt kräftig ihr Gesicht; seinen Schwung bekommt das Wasser aus ihren eigenen Händen.

Geräusche, Laute, die sich nicht einfach voneinander unterscheiden lassen. Plötzlich der Pfeifton ...

Ausatmen. Ein Schritt – und noch einer – haben dahin geführt. In der Luft ist ihr Körper gestreckt; die rechte Hand befindet sich auf Augenhöhe, in einem Versuch die Taucherbrille vor dem Wasser-Kontakt zu schützen. Die linke Hand – ähnlich angespannt – sorgt dafür, dass die swimming cap an ihrer Stelle bleibt. Beide Ellenbogen nähern sich und daraus entsteht eine Art Dreieck.[1]

     ... und danach dieses S p l a s h

Füße berühren das Wasser und es saugt wie ein Magnet den gesamten Körper auf einmal nach unten. Die Schwerkraft schafft den Platz im Wasser für diesen und noch sieben weitere Körper, die getrennt nebeneinander schweben werden. Jetzt berühren ihre Zehen die raue Oberfläche der Bodenfließen und sie stößt sich davon ab. Einatmen.

Aufregung, Adrenalin, Silence aber nicht Ruhe. Sie nährt sich der Wand schnell. So viele Gedanken bis zu dem Punkt, wo ihre beiden Hände die metallene Stange des Startblocks festhalten. Wird der Bund des Badeanzugs da bleiben? Hoffentlich rutschen meine Füße an dieser gelben Wand nicht. „It's my life and it's now or never". Ah, lenk' dich nicht ab, stay focused.

Kurzer Pfeifton: Vorwarnung. Acht Körper, eine Position: sie sehen aus wie eine Kurve, die noch nicht aufgerichtet wurde.
Take your marks. L a n g s a m a u s a t m e n. **Beep**. Schnell einatmen. Acht entfaltete Bogen in der Luft und danach nichts. Silence aber nicht Ruhe. Ihr Körper ist gestreckt, sie bewegt sich fast parallel zu dem Boden mit einem leichten Neigungswinkel nach oben. Ihre an den Ohren verbundenen Arme zeigen ihr, wohin sie gehen muss. Ihre Fußbewegungen bilden leichte Kräuselungen und unregelmäßig geformte Luftblasen befreien sich aus ihrer Nase.

Geräusche, Laute, die sich nicht einfach voneinander unterscheiden lassen. Eine sehr bunte Masse an Figuren, eine gerade Linie, die in regelmäßigem Takt auftaucht und noch eine von der anderen Seite: zwei Paddel in der Farbe ihrer Haut. Auf einem von ihnen ist etwas mit Marker Geschriebenes leicht sichtbar; eine Herz-Person hat es vermutlich kurz skizziert.

---

[1] Wie viel Zeit ist dazwischen gegangen? Jetzt muss ich das nochmal machen, um mir diese Körperhaltung wieder ins Gedächtnis zu rufen... Sie springt auf ihre blaue Yoga-Matte, die von gestern noch auf dem Boden liegt.

In regelmäßigen Abständen d^r$_{eh}$^{e}n ^{si}$_{ch}$ ^{a}$_l$^{e} Körper für ein paar Hundertstelsekunden, kehren dann aber in ihre Ordnung zurück. Das Atmen synchronisiert sich mit den abwechselnden Handbewegungen: ein und aus . 2 3 4 ein, aus aus aus 1.

Zum letzten Mal kurz die Rückenfähnchen sehend, weiß sie, dass die letzten 5 Meter schon angefangen haben. Und danach ihre rechte Hand kräftig auf dem gelben Touchpad. Blick direkt auf die digitale Uhr: ihre Zeit und ihre Positionierung unter den anderen sieben Körpern.
A u s a t m e n .
Schwimmbrille und swimming cap sind jetzt an ihrem Handgelenk zusammen mit ihrem Haargummi. Ihre losen Haare werden sofort nass, als sie unter den Schwimmbahnen hindurch zur Seitenwand taucht.

Namen werden aus den Lautsprechern aufgerufen: Das nächste 100m Rückenschwimmen beginnt bald. Gesichter werden sichtbar, Gefühle werden geweckt, ihr Blick sucht nach bestimmten Personen; ein paar fehlen.

Dort, bevor sich ihre Füße wieder eine menschliche Bewegung aneignen, atmet sie ein.

~ *Rika Sakalak*

SCHLAFITTCHEN

Dachtet ihr Zaraffel etwa, ihr kämt einfach so davon? In jeder Ausgabe nehmen wir uns hier ein Mitglied vor, und stellen es zur Rede.

In dieser Ausgabe geht es Tim an Kragen, der uns davon berichtet, wie er zum Schreiben kam, was das Verfassen persönlicher Texte von journalistischen Artikeln für ihn abhebt und welche therapeutische Funktion das Schreiben für ihn erfüllt.

Cognitive Literary Therapy: Zaraffel Interviews Tim Redfern

Zaraffel: Tim, I know that you have been writing for many years now and that writing has a special place in your life. Could you elaborate on this a little?

Tim: *Sure. I always enjoyed writing as a child and writing stories in tandem with my friends was my main hobby when I was 14 and 15. We would take turns to write a few paragraphs at a time, allowing the story to develop spontaneously without planning. It was really a lot of fun.*

When I was 16, however, writing took on a new dimension for me. At that time, I entered into a depressive phase that lasted for most of 2008, and while I didn't tell many people about what I was going through, it was a really rough time. At some point I began to write down what was going through my mind. I quickly filled up many pages with thousands and thousands of words in a sort of self-analysis. Articulating my thoughts on the page helped me to analyse them with a new perspective, and eventually helped me to break out of negative thought cycles. It was a sort of self-facilitated cognitive analytical therapy, I guess. I always felt better afterwards, and it enabled me to better understand my thoughts and make a productive plan to move forward. That simple writing exercise improved my mental state immensely after months of unhappiness.

That was thirteen years ago, but ever since then I have maintained that exercise of writing in order to analyse my own thoughts, to process my own experiences and inner life. That is the background to my love of writing, or at least how it has played a special role in my life. Nowadays my writing habits are different: I write either creative pieces or exploratory essays intended for publication, not just for private journaling. Nonetheless, for me, the writing process is always an opportunity to process and better understand what is going on inside my own mind.

Zaraffel: Does your writing connect a lot to your personal experience?

Tim: *Yes, absolutely. As I mentioned, for a long time I wrote as a way of processing my own thoughts and experiences in a constructive way. Since 2019 I have been writing articles for publication, but these articles also tend to reflect topics or experiences that I have encountered personally, or which have at least preoccupied my thinking on some intense level. In this second issue of Zaraffel, for example, my text 'Lines' draws heavily upon my own experience of addiction, which I wanted to explore creatively. The feeling of being divided against oneself, and the experience of 'negotiating' with one's own addiction, is something I know quite intimately. My other piece, 'Encounters,' is also based on real events. Drawing on my own experiences for inspiration makes writing an intensely personal process for me, and sharing these experiences through stories is, of course, a bit intimidating – but, I suppose, that is what makes self-expression so rewarding.*

Zaraffel: Your interest, which can be seen especially in the first edition of Zaraffel in your text *Mysticism and Political Transformation: A Prologue*, seems to lie in authoring essays. What draws you to this particular genre?

Tim: *Essays are usually what I have the most energy and inspiration for. I often become fascinated by specific topics or ideas, and from this initial fascination I find the energy to dive into the process of exploration through reading and writing. By writing about a topic, the explorative process* *becomes iterative, and I quickly see where my knowledge is lacking and can then direct my reading accordingly. In some cases I start writing an essay just as I begin to explore a topic, since the writing process provides me with a structure for reading and reflection. Aside from that, after so many years as a student, essay writing just comes naturally.*

Zaraffel: Now, referring to the same essay I mentioned, I would like to ask you about the part, where you claim that the capitalistic "machine" has us in its grasp, unless we can learn to refrain from consuming. Do you believe that mysticism can influence us regarding that? In what way?

Tim: *Well, that is what I am trying to explore and figure out. I think there is an urgent need to explore any kinds of influences that can help break the dominant position of consumerist culture. Education by itself does not seem to be sufficient, since more educated societies typically become more consumption-oriented, and the most highly educated social classes tend to be the worst offenders when it comes to wealth accumulation and overconsumption. Of course, education is still extremely important, but I think we also need to look for influences that can shift peoples' priorities at the level of values or consciousness in a deeper sense.*

I have always found it interesting how, compared to mainstream forms of religion, mystical traditions have often cultivated a radical political outlook and an ethos of simple, non-consumerist living. Chassidic Judaism, for example, which swept through the Jewish communities of Eastern Europe in the 17th and 18th centuries as a mass movement, was a popularisation of mystical practices drawn from the Lurianic Kabbalah. It promoted a way of life which is simple, community-oriented, and non-consumerist, along with systems of mutual aid that were independent of state structures.

In many ways, the social principles of Chassidism had a lot in common with anarchism. Likewise, the Anabaptists of Western Europe were a mystical community who practiced a radical lifestyle of sharing and simplicity. In the Münster Rebellion, when Anabaptists tried to create a new society in Germany, they declared that all property was to be held in common and redistributed wealth to the poor. The Quakers, a mystical sect from England, are a similar example, having adopted simplicity and egalitarianism as central principles of their lifestyle. These all provide interesting comparisons to mainstream religious traditions, which usually lacked both the mystical elements and the radical political or social tendencies. Or, insofar as those mainstream traditions contained mystical elements, these were confined to monasteries which, of course, were communities of simple living, close to nature and with minimal consumption.

My thesis is that there is something inherent in the nature of mystical, transcendent or ecstatic experience that causes this shift in values. These experiences and practices, including when they occur at the communal level, seem to trigger a radical change in perspective and priorities. I do not think the solution to our social and ecological problems is a mass wave of mystical conversions, but I am curious as to what this dimension of experience, rooted in ecstasy and transcendence, can offer us on a larger scale – the scale of society at large, the polis. And to investigate this, I decided to look at cases where mysticism has intersected with radical politics throughout history.

Zaraffel: It seems to me a bold idea to connect politics and mysticism, as you yourself point out in your essay. And I also know that you intend to continue the series. So, without spoiling anything to come, I (and I am sure, our

readers as well) am curious what lead you in this particular direction.

Tim: *When I was studying politics at university, I read Tim Jackson's Prosperity Without Growth. He was one of the first thinkers to make the idea of de-growth popular in the 2010s. He argues that current consumption patterns are inherently unsustainable, even if we shift to renewable energy, and that the only solution is to literally lower material consumption – and therefore also production – across the economy. Jackson points out that one of the chief difficulties in achieving this goal lies in the consumerist culture of modern society. As long as this mentality and culture remain dominant, any hopes of reducing consumption are naïve.*

At the same time, I was reading a lot about religion, mysticism, and the science of ecstatic experiences. The philosopher Jules Evan's book The Art of Losing Control was a watershed for me in that respect and showed me the importance of the ecstatic in the scheme of human values. Bringing these two concerns together, I wondered whether a post-religious spirituality or a rediscovered 'accesses' to mystical experience could offer a new approach to the problem of overconsumption and consumerist culture in affluent, industrial societies. That, I guess, is how I got started on this trajectory.

Zaraffel: Returning to the current edition, you surprised us with a story rather than an essay. What brought about this shift? And how do you feel about it?

Tim: *The short answer is that that is what I felt inspired to write this time around. The last few months have been rough; this seemingly endless lockdown and lack of activity outside of work has left me fairly burnt out and frustrated, and I know I am not alone in this regard. I did not want to push my-*

self to research complex topics while I was so lacking in energy, so instead I allowed inspiration to simply direct the writing process as it came to me. It felt good to write a story after years of writing only essays. That surprised me, but it was also refreshing. I guess there was something within me that needed to be expressed in this manner and it was just the right time for it to emerge.

~ Das Interview führte Mirona C.

60